"I'll get you for this.
Nobody makes a fool out of me."

His dark eyebrows arched wickedly as one of his hands moved threateningly down to the curve of her bottom.

"I'm trembling," she said wryly.

"You should be. Why didn't you tell me before?"

"I tried to, several times, but you absolutely refused to listen. Anyway, I didn't want to spoil your fun. You seemed to take such pleasure in trying to intimidate me with your TV program. 'I'm going to lead you to a very public stake...and then I'm going to burn you!'" she quoted, mimicking his intonation perfectly.

"You're in big trouble, witch," he repeated with a grin. "For a solid week you've played havoc with my peace of mind with this little act of yours." His roughly sensual voice sent shivers through her. "Now I'm going to have my revenge..."

Dear Reader:

Romance readers today have more choice among books than ever before. But with so many titles to choose from, deciding what to select becomes increasingly difficult.

At SECOND CHANCE AT LOVE we try to make that decision easy for you — by publishing romances of the highest quality every month. You can confidently buy any SECOND CHANCE AT LOVE romance and know it will provide you with solid romantic entertainment.

Sometimes you buy romances by authors whose work you've previously read and enjoyed — which makes a lot of sense. You're being sensible . . . and careful . . . to look for satisfaction where you've found it before.

But if you're *too* careful, you risk overlooking exceptional romances by writers whose names you don't immediately recognize. These first-time authors may be the stars of tomorrow, and you won't want to miss any of their books! At SECOND CHANCE AT LOVE, many writers who were once "new" are now the most popular contributors to the line. So trying a new writer at SECOND CHANCE AT LOVE isn't really a risk at all. Every book we publish must meet our rigorous standards — whether it's by a popular "regular" or a newcomer.

In the months to come, we urge you to watch for these names — Linda Raye, Karen Keast, Betsy Osborne, Dana Daniels, and Cinda Richards. All are dazzling new writers, an elite few whose books are destined to become "keepers." We think you'll be delighted and excited by their first books with us!

Look, too, for romances by writers with whom you're already warmly familiar: Jeanne Grant, Ann Cristy, Linda Barlow, Elissa Curry, Jan Mathews, and Liz Grady, among many others.

Best wishes,

Ellen Edwards

Ellen Edwards, Senior Editor
SECOND CHANCE AT LOVE
The Berkley Publishing Group
200 Madison Avenue
New York, N.Y. 10016

BEWITCHED

LINDA BARLOW

A
SECOND CHANCE AT LOVE
BOOK

Other Second Chance at Love books by
Linda Barlow

BEGUILED #168
FLIGHTS OF FANCY #188

First edition published October 1984

First printing

"Second Chance at Love" and the butterfly emblem are trademarks belonging to Jove Publications, Inc.

Printed in the United States of America

Second Chance at Love books are published by
The Berkley Publishing Group
200 Madison Avenue, New York, NY 10016

To my parents, Babs and Bob Barlow, who have been living "happily ever after" for more than forty years—truly the most romantic couple I know!

Chapter

1

SHE COULD FEEL his eyes on her. She'd been disturbed by it all evening. Her awareness of him was manifested by a tingling at the back of her neck when he was behind her and a heaviness in her breasts when he was in front of her. He was usually in front.

There was something menacingly dark about him. He had black hair and charcoal-gray eyes. Even his clothes were dark: He wore a deep-gray sweater over a pair of black trousers, enhancing the monochromatic effect. Yet, in the rare moments when she allowed herself to look up and meet his eyes, Bret felt flashes of color zing through her: vibrant crimson, bright, angry orange. She'd never known anything like it before.

"Scorpio," said a light, British-accented voice in her ear.

1

"What?" She looked up, finding her friend Graham Hamilton beside her, his mercurial mouth curved in a smile. He had returned to the table in the corner of the Beacon Hill apartment where he and Bret were serving as astrologer and psychic for the entertainment of thirty or forty guests. Psychic indeed, thought Bret sardonically. That was a laugh.

Graham lounged over the arm of her easy chair, handing her a glass of white wine. "Your brooding admirer," Graham went on, flicking one hand in the direction of the man Bret was beginning to think of as her dark angel. "Ten to one he's a Scorpio. Powerful physique, hawklike features, heavy brows, intense eyes. Sexual magnetism, too; that goes without saying. Better watch out, Bret, luv. He could be trouble."

Bret didn't argue; she knew trouble when she saw it. "Who is he?"

"You're the psychic, my dear. You tell *me*. I'm only an unenlightened astrologer."

"Very funny," Bret said, half serious, half laughing. "I'm putting a spell on you the moment we get out of here, Graham. I could strangle you for suckering me into this charade. Madame Bret indeed!" She gestured toward the fortune-telling paraphernalia laid on the table in front of her: tarot cards, palmistry charts, *I Ching* sticks, and Graham's astrological tables. "About the only thing we don't have is a crystal ball."

Graham grinned. "Concentrate on him, luv," he ordered, nodding at the brooder. "Tell me the time and place of his birth."

"Don't be absurd."

"If he's a Scorpio, you and he could be very compatible, you know. You're both water signs. Great empathy is possible, and the sex would be terrific. You could use a little terrific sex, darling, couldn't you?"

"I can live without it," Bret said firmly.

"On the other hand," Graham went on thoughtfully,

darting another glance at the stranger, "it could be a disaster. He would try to dominate you, and a yielding little fish like you could easily be swallowed up and crushed."

"A yielding little fish?" she repeated, quirking her eyebrows at him. "Come on, Graham. Sometimes I think astrology's a pail of garbage."

"It's the one true path to enlightenment," he said solemnly. "And it has the virtue of being scientific as well."

Bret pushed away the arm Graham insisted on slinging around her waist. "There are many paths to enlightenment," she told him archly.

He deliberately replaced the arm. "I'm still waiting for one of those paths to lead you into my bedroom," he murmured, raising his eyebrows in a mock leer.

"No chance, Graham. You once admitted to me that our charts decree we'd be hopelessly incompatible in bed."

"Maybe astrology *is* a pail of garbage," he said ruefully.

Bret laughed, then sobered as she cast another look at her tarot cards. Once again she was surprised at herself for agreeing to help Graham out this evening by masquerading as a psychic. The only reason she'd gotten away with it so far, she suspected, was that the guests were fun-loving and sophisticated and no one was taking her seriously.

"Do you really have a colleague named Madame Olivia who's down with the flu?" she asked. "Since when have you been working as a team with a psychic?"

"I only worked with her once, actually," he admitted. "A really spooky lady. She not only has a sixth sense, but a seventh, eighth, and ninth as well."

"Well, the only thing my sixth sense tells me is that I'm probably going to be denounced as a fraud."

"Nonsense, luv. Don't keep underrating your abilities. You're a professional actress, and a damn good one.

Besides, I've told you you have true psychic powers. Pisces is the most mystical sign in the zodiac, and your mother's a famous medium."

"Don't remind me," she groaned. "When can we leave?"

"Not for at least an hour. We've got four or five more readings after this break is over. Want another glass of wine?"

"Yes! Bring the bottle."

She and Graham were officially on one of the evening's three breaks, during which they were supposed to be regenerating their psychic powers. Wine wasn't going to help, though, Bret told herself wryly as she recalled her mother's confirmed belief in the mystical powers of herbal teas. Thank God her mother wasn't here to see her now. She'd be ecstatic to discover that her only daughter was finally following in her footsteps!

Playing idly with her tarot deck, Bret watched Graham "regenerate" by mixing with the guests—the women in particular. His old-world English charm, combined with his slender elegance and his blond good looks, always seemed to bring him ample success in that endeavor, and his knowledge of astrology added to his appeal. Like Bret, he was an actor—a member of her company, in fact—and he was accustomed to playing the role of the elegant Briton charmed by American beauty and high spirits. Women fell all over Graham, but Bret had been friends with him for so long that her own knees never buckled in his presence.

Her knees never buckled for any man, she assured herself as she snuck a quick glance in the direction of the dark-eyed stranger. Maybe he'd be gone? No such luck. His lean, well-formed body was still propped casually against the opposite wall. Automatically she noted his lazy grace, the aura of dynamic physical power he radiated. He was not the most handsome man she had

ever seen—his features were angular rather than clas-
sic—but there was an exciting earthiness about him. His
hair was black and wavy, a trifle long over the collar—
the sort of hair a woman longed to sink her fingers into.
Hmm. Her knees were definitely beginning to feel a little
weak.

Because of the way he was lounging against the wall,
with one hand thrust aggressively into a trouser pocket,
Bret could see that his stomach was trim, his hips and
thighs tautly free of extra flesh. She supposed he must
exercise regularly to stay so fit. A line or two on his face
and the hint of gray around his temples confirmed that
he was on the far side of thirty-five.

And he was certainly persistent! He was still staring
at her in a strange and rather malevolent manner. Deliberately she met his gaze and smiled. He didn't smile
back, but she saw his eyes widen, as if in shock.

Maybe he was mentally deranged. Or drugged. Maybe
he was some kind of weirdo who was engaging in a lurid
fantasy about abducting and ravishing her. He looked
like a ravisher, with that rugged jaw and those dark,
penetrating eyes. Unlike Graham, who slyly cajoled and
gently seduced women, this man, Bret knew intuitively,
would simply take what he wanted, and to hell with the
consequences.

Looking away, she shuffled the tarot cards. Damn
him; he was making her nervous!

When Graham returned to their corner a couple of
minutes later, he seemed a trifle subdued. He sat down
beside her and nervously scanned the guests. "I just heard
a disturbing rumor, luv. Someone told me that D. D.
Haggarty's here tonight. You know, that investigative
reporter turned TV producer who's made a name for
himself recently by rounding up and exposing fakes?"

"Fakes?" The word came out in a croak.

"Everything from falsely labelled 'natural foods' to

UFO reports. He's a real crusader in the old muckraker tradition. His TV show is a big hit this year—sort of a local version of *Sixty Minutes*."

"Dear God, yes, I've heard of him. Didn't he run a piece about Myra Kelley, that medium who used to be a friend of my mother's?"

"Yeah, I think so. I didn't see it myself, but I heard Haggarty's minions really worked her over. Said she faked seances and ripped off grieving widows. He's got a thing against psychics, spiritualists in particular."

"And he undoubtedly eats bogus fortune-tellers like me for supper." She moaned. "Graham—"

"I know. This whole setup was a stupid idea. It's just that I'd promised Marilyn, and I couldn't bear to disappoint her when—"

"Yes, yes," Bret interrupted, not about to listen once again to the touching story of Graham's blind friend, Marilyn, the hostess of tonight's party, who had "given her solemn word of honor" to all her friends that she would have an astrologer and a psychic present. The token fees Graham was charging for "readings" were being donated to the National Foundation for the Blind.

Graham was searching the room, examining each of the fashionably attired guests. "I don't see him. Maybe he won't notice us."

"What does he look like?"

"I'm not sure. He doesn't actually appear on the program; he's the head writer and producer. I did see a picture of him once. I've been trying to pick him out ever since I heard he was here."

Bret's eyes flew to her black-clad nemesis. He was still leaning against the wall, quietly sipping a drink. And he was still staring at her. "Oh, no. He's probably our Scorpio brooder," she said with a shiver. "He looks as though he's been contemplating my ruin all evening."

"No, Scorpio is too young. Haggarty's fiftyish and balding, if I remember correctly. Besides, that guy is too busy contemplating your body to contemplate your ruin. Smart man," he added, leaning over the side of her chair to run a finger down the pearly buttons of her green silk blouse.

"Graham!" She struggled against him, exasperated. She'd known Graham too long to be overly offended. He was a good friend, but whenever he drank he had more hands than a Hindu goddess.

"The lady doesn't seem to want your attentions," said a deep voice from just above their heads. Bret looked up. The Scorpio brooder had finally proved himself capable of motion—startlingly swift motion, at that. And the latent aggression Bret had sensed in him had come to the fore; his fists were clenched, and he looked as if he were about to toss Graham across the room.

"Bloody hell, an old-fashioned chivalrous knight to the rescue," said Graham, slowly removing his hand from Bret's blouse. He gave the man a careless once-over, then shot a mischievous look at Bret. He rose to his feet. "She doesn't require aid, I assure you. I'm only a poor misguided astrologer, but *she* is a witch." Then he winked at Bret and rejoined the other guests.

Great, thought Bret. A witch. Graham was making a teasing reference to her current role in the New Cambridge Repertory's production of *Macbeth;* she was playing one of the three witches. But unless the Scorpio brooder was an aficionado of small independent Boston theater groups, he wouldn't get the joke.

With some trepidation she met the stranger's eyes. Once again she felt the strange sensation of colors flashing: golds, scarlets, deep, arcing blues. Her next breath came with difficulty.

"A witch?" the low-timbred, silky voice repeated. "Yes, that I can well believe." The charcoal eyes flicked over her, taking in at close range everything he had studied for so long from across the room.

For an instant Bret saw herself through his eyes: her

pale complexion and large green eyes accented by her midnight-black hair; her slender form clad in the soft green blouse and a multicolored skirt that swirled around her legs; her breasts taut against her blouse, aching pleasurably, as if he had touched them. She made a nervous gesture, pressing her fingers to her throat, as he spoke again.

"They used to burn witches, didn't they? Tell me, witch"—he spoke the word caressingly, sending the colors storming through her again—"have you no fear of the flames?"

She answered as if hypnotized, which was exactly how she felt. "I have a recurring dream of a fire that threatens me. I wake up trembling."

His eyes narrowed, and displeasure showed plainly on his face. Bret's trancelike feeling vanished. What was she, crazy, answering him like that? This fortune-telling charade was beginning to affect her normally down-to-earth personality. "Who are you?" she demanded. "Why have you been glaring at me all evening?"

He smiled ruefully. For a moment the smile softened his features, making him seem a little less of a devil. "You noticed me glaring? I thought I was being discreet."

She smiled back, warming instantly to his faintly self-deprecatory tone. She noted again that he was attractive, in a predatory sort of way. His dark eyes radiated masculine confidence—too much of it for her taste. Not the sort of man she'd ever care to get involved with, but interesting, nevertheless.

"Are you here for a psychic reading?" she asked, pretending to consult her list, although she knew full well he was not one of the guests who had signed up. "What's your name?"

His smile faded. "Surely you can reach into my brain and pull out my name, like a rabbit from a hat. Go ahead, witch. Try."

"I don't do tricks," she snapped.

His heavy black eyebrows rose. "No?" he said softly.
"Pity." She felt his gaze burning the silk off her breasts
and realized too late the double meaning of her words.
It didn't take any psychic ability to recognize the sensual
intent in him. Arrogant devil. Definitely not her type.

"If you don't want a reading, perhaps you'd like to
contribute something to the National Foundation for the
Blind anyway?"

Surprising her, he sat down in the chair opposite her
and placed his arm on the table between them, palm up
but hidden in a clenched fist. "I'd be happy to. But like
everyone else here tonight, I'm intrigued by the possibility of getting something in return. Go ahead, witch,"
he challenged. "Open my hand; open my heart."

All of a sudden she was wildly curious to look into
his palm. Eagerness shot through her. She knew a bit
about palmistry—she could hardly grow up as the daughter of a famous crackpot medium without learning *something*—and she could lay out the tarot deck. Without
these minimal talents she never would have agreed to
help Graham out tonight.

She knew enough, surely, to fool this cocksure
stranger. After all, she told herself bracingly, she *was* a
professional actress. This performance ought to be a piece
of cake. So why was her heart beating like a kettledrum?

He was waiting, his fist clenched on the table between
them. "Do you want me to cross your palm with silver
first?" he asked sarcastically.

She had a fuzzy image of the injured paw of a jungle
beast—of the man across from her as fiercely predatory
on the surface but tender deep inside—pierced by the
same thorn of loneliness that tormented her. She felt as
if she were blacking out, and the room tilted. The wine,
she told herself.

"Your name is Daniel," she heard herself say. "First
or last, I don't know, but one of your names is Daniel."

His eyes opened wider for an instant before the lids

half closed, hiding his reaction. "Very clever. Although why I'm still so surprised when people recognize me is more than I can tell. You're going to have to do a lot better than that to impress me, green eyes."

"You mean your name *is* Daniel?" she gasped, totally shocked.

He smiled unpleasantly. "Don't play games with me, witch. Of course it is."

"Dear heavens," she muttered. Could it be that she . . . her mother had always said . . . no. Get hold of yourself, Bret. It was a lucky guess, that's all.

Daniel. She liked the name.

"I'm Bret," she said, giving him a shaky smile.

"I know your name, Miss Carter, all too well."

"Mrs. Kingsley," she corrected him sharply and automatically. She stared at him in puzzlement. Carter was her birth name, which she hadn't used in over five years. Even on stage she'd always called herself Bret Kingsley. "Have we met?"

The fist on the table between them seemed to clench a little more. "You're married?" He sounded so shocked at the idea that Bret was taken aback. She was tempted to lie, intuiting that the sensual threat in this man would be reined in immediately if he believed she was married. She knew instinctively that he would not harass another man's wife.

"I'm a widow," she clarified. "But it's *your* psyche we're probing, Daniel, not mine."

"How long?" he demanded, ignoring her last remark.

"What?"

"How long have you been a widow?"

Once again she was surprised. The usual response to her widowhood was a polite statement like, "I'm sorry," or "You're so young—how sad." Not that most new acquaintances felt any real sympathy, she reminded herself. How could they? They didn't know her, and they hadn't known Arthur. At least Daniel didn't pretend. "It's been three years now," she replied.

"And you still say it so mournfully? Such devotion."

A seed of anger burst inside her. How dare he mock her grief? What did he know about devotion to a man you still missed and would always remember with love? She raised her green eyes to his charcoal ones, feeling the sparks sing back and forth between them. "Look, I didn't come here to be baited and snarled at. If you want a reading, fine; if you don't, kindly take yourself back to the same corner where you've spent the evening so far."

"Open my hand, Bret," he ordered softly.

Her anger faded, and she felt a rush of blood to her head as she saw a riot of vibrant jungle colors—and a hole gaping in front of her, as dark and black as any hell. Suddenly she was afraid to move, to take a step in any direction, and most of all, to touch him. But his eyes had darkened to near-black, compelling her more powerfully than she'd ever been compelled in her life. Her fingers covered his.

His hand was warm. Its heat communicated itself to her, radiating through her like a sunburst. She felt herself flush, and hoped he wouldn't notice, but his eyes wouldn't release hers. There was magic in those dark-pool depths, a strong, hypnotizing pull on all her senses. Who was he? she wondered in fear and mystery. A real psychic? A sorcerer from another world?

Bret tore her gaze away, calling on all her reserves of calm. Her imagination was running away with her. She was tired and overly fanciful. She never should have allowed Graham to talk her into this. She ought to get up right this minute and leave.

But Daniel's flesh was warm beneath her fingertips, and she couldn't resist a look into his palm. Gently she pried open his fingers. His hand was nicely shaped, firm and masculine, its palm richly covered with clearly defined lines.

"Your hand is ruled by fire, the most passionate of the four elements," she noted as she compared the relative length of his fingers to his palm.

"What's that supposed to mean?"

If there was anything to palmistry, it meant that he was emotional and intuitive—a man of energy who lived life to the fullest. Yet she knew that already, simply from looking into his eyes.

Without answering, she turned his hand over and examined the shape of his nails, then turned it back to compare the individual fingers. He had a strong, forceful thumb—a good sign. The mount of Jupiter, from which sprang the index finger, governor of earthly ambitions, was particularly well developed.

"Well?" he drawled. "Are you estimating how many years I've got left on my lifeline?"

"I'm not even looking at the lines yet. The shape of the hand, the position of the fingers and their relative lengths, and the condition of the fleshy mounts beneath the fingers are at least as important as the lines."

"Is that so? And what do these marvelous signposts of personality tell you about me?"

For some reason his sarcasm was beginning to amuse her. She told herself not to laugh; he would undoubtedly be offended. Then she wondered why on earth she should care if he was. "You are dynamic, energetic, and determined to succeed in whatever you undertake," she declared. "The strength of Jupiter—your index finger—confirms that you have the ability to be both a leader and an innovator, and the willpower to follow through." She tilted her head a little to one side as she thoughtfully added, "I would even go so far as to say that when you set your mind on something, you are driven to achieve it, no matter what the cost."

"That's true," he agreed readily. "But I don't believe you're getting it from my blasted index finger."

Shrugging casually, she touched the fleshy mount of the moon, on the percussion of his hand. "This side of your hand suggests that there's a conflict going on inside you between reason and intuition, logic and imagination. Note the lines of the head and heart." She traced them on his palm, highly conscious of the heat of his skin beneath her fingertips. "Both lines are firm and deep, but the headline swings down into the mount of the moon—imagination—while the heartline moves upward toward Jupiter—practicality."

She raised her eyes to meet his. "A lot of conflict, Daniel. A very interesting hand."

He raised his eyebrows and smiled abstractedly, and she had the momentary impression that despite his skepticism, he was intrigued. Then his strong thumb curved down over her fingers and began softly massaging them. "Tell me about my love life, witch," he invited.

His touch wreaked havoc with her heartbeat, and she knew she ought to snatch her hand away. But something about him challenged her, dared her to take risks that would have seemed unthinkable only a few minutes ago. Deliberately she ran her crimson-polished nails over the base of his thumb. It was fleshy, and the semicircular line known as the girdle of Venus showed clearly under the middle finger, or the mount of Saturn. "You are an extremely sensual man," she said. "A man of unruly passions. Sex is important to you. But the nature of fire is to burn brightly and consume, leaving ashes in its wake."

"So let my lovers beware—is that what you're intimating?"

"Yes," she said, a tad irritated at the satisfaction he seemed to be deriving from this. It was probably exactly what a rapacious male like Daniel wanted to hear. "But I wouldn't get too cocky if I were you. Your heartline is ragged at the beginning, but it deepens into one smoothly flowing groove, suggesting that you just might end up channeling all your sensual energy into a single relationship someday."

"Ah, your first prediction. I'm going to meet a beautiful stranger, I suppose, and fall madly and permanently in love with her?"

"Don't put words into my mouth. I don't make predictions. You make your own future. It grows out of your character."

This was a slip, she knew—the actress of Shakespearean tragedy speaking, not the psychic. She hoped Daniel wouldn't catch it, but he immediately pounced.

"A fortune-teller who believes in free will? Now that *is* original."

"I'm not really a fortune-teller," she admitted, sick of the pretense. So what if he found her out? Somebody was bound to; she'd known that from the start. She pushed his hand away. "I'm an actress."

"All fortune-tellers are actresses, Ms.—sorry, *Mrs.*—Kingsley, so don't waste your touching confessions on me. I'm not as gullible as the people who usually sit across the table from you."

Bret heard his words and laughed, a spontaneous burst of gaiety. So much for being honest about her profession. He'd drawn his own conclusions about her, and that was that. "No," she agreed when she managed to control herself again. "You're much too self-assured to be gullible, Daniel. You have strong opinions, and you make harsh judgments. Tolerance of other people's foibles is not your long suit, is it?"

His eyes met hers; then he smiled. Once again the smile revealed that there was more to him than his superficial arrogance would seem to indicate. "And you, my lovely witch, are very perceptive. Yes, I am opinionated, judgmental, and intolerant. I'm am also aggressive and hot-tempered. But I have some good qualities, too."

"You admit your faults. That in itself is a good quality," she answered softly.

"I'm honest," he said intensely. "And I'm constant. When I make a friend, the tie endures for life."

"And when you make an enemy?" she couldn't stop herself from asking.

His dark eyes glowed into hers. "Chalk up a few more points on the negative side of the ledger. Like my lovers, let my enemies beware: I will hold a grudge for years and hound them to death."

She shivered. She believed him.

"You're reluctant to make predictions for me," he added after a brief silence. "Let me give it a try." He raised his eyes to hers again. "I will leave this party with a dark, mysterious, and utterly feminine stranger." His fingers closed over hers, sending waves of heat throughout her body. "I'll develop such an obsession with a certain beautiful witch that it's almost going to make me forget my intentions regarding her."

Bret wanted to look away, but he held her mesmerized.

"Almost," he repeated, his voice deceptively mild. "But, like a stern old Puritan, I know my duty. Witchcraft cannot be allowed to flourish. Obsession or no, I'm going to have to break all her spells."

She jerked her hand away as all the danger she'd felt in him suddenly coalesced. "Who are you?" she demanded.

"You're a witch, Bret," he said in a harshly caressing tone. "And I'm a witch-hunter. Daniel David Haggarty is my full name, and I intend to see that your tricks are discredited forever. I'm going to lead you to a very public stake, Bret Carter Kingsley, and then I'm going to burn you."

Chapter

2

BRET'S IMMEDIATE REACTION to Daniel's threat was to stare round-eyed at him for a moment, then burst into peals of delighted laughter. "You're making a big mistake," she finally managed. He looked so surprised to see her laughing that she giggled even more, bringing several of the guests wandering over in their direction, clearly wondering what was so funny.

"I'm damned if I see anything to be so riproaringly amused about," Daniel growled at her. But there was a sparkle in his eyes as he watched her laugh, and Bret sensed that on some deep level her refusal to take him seriously appealed to him.

"You will when I explain. You see, I'm here this evening only as a favor to a friend, and—"

"You don't usually perform at private parties?" he

interrupted. "No, I imagine not. And for charity, too. I suppose you far prefer to work in the privacy of your own home, where you can control the environment and set up the bigger tricks: the mysterious voices from the Other Side, the astral manifestations, cheesecloth ectoplasm, and so on?"

Bret's eyebrows rose in an exaggerated gesture of continuing mirth. He was determined not to alter his initial impression of her. She supposed she couldn't really blame him: First she'd billed herself as a psychic; then Graham had declared her to be a witch; and just now she'd charged right ahead, reading his palm and analyzing his character. If it was true that he hated psychics and made it his business to expose frauds, naturally he'd be out to get her.

She was seized with an irresistible desire to take the formidable D. D. Haggarty down a peg. He was going to feel damn foolish when he discovered the truth about her, and in the meantime perhaps she could have a little fun with him. It would serve him right.

"I'm just reading cards and palms," she said defensively. "I'm not claiming to be a medium, for heaven's sake!"

"Fortune-tellers, witches, mediums—you're all in it together. Cheating people, preying on their superstitions. In some cases you even cause grave psychological harm." He glared at her, his dark eyes spitting fire. "You with your sixth sense. Do you realize that several of the guests here tonight don't even have a fifth sense? But you are 'sighted,' aren't you. You are 'gifted'—"

"Darling," Graham's voice interrupted. He had unobstrusively made his way to their side, and Bret looked up at him in amused relief. "I've just found out which one D. D. Haggarty is."

"So have I." Bret let out an elaborate sigh. "You told me he was fiftyish and balding."

To her astonishment, Daniel laughed at this descrip-

tion, a rich, full-bodied laugh not unlike her own. Bret
shot him a reconsidering look from under her eyelashes.
Until this moment she would have characterized him as
dour and humorless, much like one of the Puritans he
had compared himself to. "It must have been that photo
in the *Globe*," he said. "Mislabeled. It should have said
'from right to left' instead of 'from left to right.' I was
the sexy, good-looking one."

"Opinionated, judgmental, intolerant, *and* egotisti-
cal," said Bret. She smiled wryly at Graham. "You see
what you got me into? He's threatening to burn me at
the stake." She turned her gaze back to Daniel. "Burn
Graham instead. He deserves it."

Haggarty was regarding her with the intent concentration a cat lavishes on an injured bird. "But it's you
I'm after, Bret," he said smoothly, making the threat into
a kind of sensual promise.

"Terrific."

"You're not intimidated by me, are you?" he went
on, tilting his head to one side as he considered this
apparently significant piece of information. "I like that."

"If I were what you think I am, I'd probably be shaking
in my shoes," she retorted. "As it is, I can afford to laugh
at you, Mr. Haggarty."

"Daniel."

"Daniel," she agreed with a slight shrug of her shoulders.

Before either of them could speak again, an elderly
woman decked out in elaborate copper jewelry came to
the table, pointing triumphantly at her watch. "This
gentleman's time is up," she said, tapping Daniel on the
shoulder. "I'm so excited, Madame Bret! I just can't wait
to hear whether or not Rudy is going to propose to me."

Bret smiled pleasantly at the woman. "Mr. Haggarty
was just leaving. Please take a seat."

Daniel rose, scowling. He was about to move away

when Bret touched his arm. He stopped, looking as electrified as she felt. "What?"

She pointed to the canister marked NATIONAL FOUNDATION FOR THE BLIND. "My fee."

If she expected annoyance, she was disappointed. He was very gracious about opening his wallet and dropping a hundred-dollar bill into the slot. She stared at it, aghast.

"I'll get my money's worth later," he promised, and he walked away.

At eleven-thirty Bret gathered up the tools of a fortune-teller's trade and looked around for Graham, who'd promised her a ride home. She found him draped over the sofa in the living room with a beautiful blind redhead, who was guiding his hand as he ran his fingertips over her bare shoulders. When Bret signaled, pointing at the door and raising her eyebrows interrogatively, he called over to her, "Wait a bit, luv. Marissa's teaching me braille."

Bret decided to take a taxi home.

As she collected her coat and said good-bye to the hostess, who gushed delightedly over Bret's spurious psychic abilities, Bret couldn't help noticing that there was no sign of Daniel David Haggarty anywhere in the apartment. He must have left. She didn't understand the odd flicker of regret she experienced. She ought to be delighted if she'd escaped the further attentions of the Scorpio brooder.

As she started down the narrow staircase of the old Beacon Hill town house, Bret ran their conversation through her mind. Why had he stared at her for so long before approaching her? How had he known her maiden name? And why had he left without making good on any of his threats? He didn't seem like the type who would back down without a confrontation. He was much too cocky for that.

She wondered why he was so down on psychics. Lots of people were skeptical, true, but Daniel seemed to carry skepticism to an extreme. Something about the subject obviously made him very angry, almost fanatical. Bret disliked fanaticism of any kind.

But in spite of this she couldn't exactly say she disliked Daniel. At least not after that unexpected laugh of his. She found him intriguing. And sexy. A simple look from those dark-charcoal eyes was more potent than an impassioned embrace from most other men. He made unruly images of naked, entwined limbs and beds with rumpled sheets flash through her mind.

She flushed slightly. He was the first man she'd thought of *that way* since Arthur's death.

As always, the memory of Arthur brought a pang. She used to wonder if the pain would ever go away, but it finally seemed to have diminished to the point where she could take pleasure in her own life again. She pictured the cheerful, good-natured face of the only man she'd ever loved—his blond hair, his warm brown eyes—and compared it with the dark, intense features of Daniel Haggarty. The two men couldn't possibly be more different. "Oh, Arthur," she said out loud, "I miss you."

"Conversing with the spirit world?" said a sardonic voice at the bottom of the stairs.

Damn. Bret stepped down the final few stairs into the dingy, badly lit lobby of the old building. D. D. Haggarty sat on a bench under the mailboxes, his long legs stretched out in front of him, blocking the exit, his dark winter coat open down the front, and his scarf loose.

"Did you think I'd gone off and left you? Impossible. Didn't you read your own cards tonight, Bret? I'm your fate."

"So far, Daniel, you've done almost as much fortune-telling tonight as I have. I'm beginning to wonder if you're really the skeptic you claim to be."

He took his time about moving his legs and rising to his feet. He proved to be several inches taller than she was, and she was tall. She didn't often have to look up so far to see a man's face. She tried to discount the pleasure this gave her. Ever since junior high school, when none of the boys had wanted to dance with her because she could rest her chin on the tops of their heads, Bret had appreciated tall males.

"I'm a skeptic all right," he assured her, his voice hardening. "You'll learn it, to your cost."

"Don't keep threatening me, please. It's rather obnoxiously macho, don't you think?"

Again he laughed. She liked the way it made his face change. He looked almost boyish, and his dark eyes sparkled. "Maybe, but machismo sometimes has its rewards. Would you permit a shy, retiring gentleman to see you home tonight?"

"No." His arrogance irritated her, but it wasn't going to be easy to resist his charm. "But that doesn't mean I'm going to permit a self-styled witch-hunter to do it. I'll see myself home."

As she moved to step out into the cold February night, D. D. Haggarty reached out and wrapped his fingers around her arm. She felt the warmth of his hand right through her wool coat. He didn't hurt her, but she sensed it was not a grip she could easily break.

"The thing about us hunters is that we don't ask permission," he whispered, his mouth somewhere near her ear. "My car is waiting right outside."

Rapidly Bret considered her options. Struggling? Acting indignant? Treating his persistence as a joke? Or simply allowing the sensations his touch engendered to sweep her away without protest?

"You're offering me a ride?" she asked casually. "How do you know I don't have my own car?"

"I asked a few questions. You came with your astrologer friend, who was too busy just now to leave with you. I made sure of that. I'm the one who introduced him to Marissa."

It figured. Bret threw him a dazzling smile, but she remembered her earlier desire to take him down a notch or two. He was really a very annoying man. "I see. Well, then, I guess I'll just have to yield to your entrapment, Machiavelli. That Porsche purring out there at the curb is your car, I presume? You live well, for a muckraker." As she spoke she slipped her hands into her gloves and adjusted the green wool scarf around her neck with as much nonchalance as possible. When she had settled it to her satisfaction she allowed her eyes to take his again. "Tell me, are you planning to burn me tonight, Daniel?" she asked. "Do I get a trial first? I can't wait to hear all the evidence against me."

His eyes glowed as he answered. "You're certainly entitled to a chance to bewitch me into silence."

"Aren't you afraid my power might prove too much for you?"

"No," he said with astonishing confidence. "I frankly doubt whether your power—or that of your mother—will stand up to my scrutiny."

Bret felt a trifle uneasy at the possibility of her mother's being exposed to a TV crusader's scrutiny. Ever since that debacle on a radio talk show a few years back when Iris Carter had calmly announced to an audience of thousands that she was a female reincarnation of Merlin the Magician, Bret had been careful to protect her flaky mother from the press. "What do you know about my mother?"

"Almost everything," he returned coolly. "I've been doing a little research for a program I'm planning on famous American mediums of the last thirty years. Your mother, naturally, is one of my subjects."

"Oh, no," Bret moaned.

"I've seen pictures of her taken when she was younger.

The resemblance between the two of you is striking. I knew she lived in a suburb of Boston, and I remembered reading somewhere that she had a daughter named Bret, but I had to stare at you for a while before I made the connection."

Good grief. That explained his odd behavior and the fact that he knew her maiden name.

"Oddly enough, none of my research has turned you up as a successor to her," he continued. His eyes swept over her again. "But you're young yet. It must take years of apprenticeship to learn how best to defraud your clients."

His misconceptions about her didn't alarm Bret anywhere near as much as his newly revealed intentions toward her mother. He *couldn't* put Iris on TV. Although she'd never actually seen the program he produced, Bret had heard enough about it to recognize the threat. D. D. Haggarty and his interviewers would make mincemeat of her mother, even though she wasn't a fraud. Bret was convinced of the validity of her mother's powers, but she knew from experience that most people were not so willing to believe. They preferred to think Iris Carter was a complete and utter madwoman.

"My mother doesn't do interviews," she informed him. "She's elderly now, and anyway, she's retired." She challenged him with her eyes as she added, "As for my being her successor, that's ridiculous. I assure you, any likeness between her and me is purely physical."

He smiled with more ease than she'd seen in him all evening. "If that's true, you, at least, have nothing to fear from me." He pushed her gently toward the doorway. "Shall we go?"

She really ought to clear up this entire misunderstanding now, Bret told herself. She ought to explain to him that in spite of her mother she herself was not a psychic, and that the closest she had ever come to dabbling in witchcraft was the role she was currently rehearsing at

New Cambridge Rep. She ought to tell him about Graham's psychic friend, and the reason she'd been at the party... and she ought *not* to get into that car with him.

But the magnetism in his eyes, combined with the pressure of his fingers on her arm, scuttled her reason. So, instead of being sensible, she said, "I really wasn't looking forward to searching for a taxi in the cold. It probably would have taken all night to get home."

"Nonsense. You would have conjured up a taxi easily. Skeptic though I am, I certainly feel as if you've put a spell on me."

She frowned. "And I feel as if I'm going to get burned."

He leaned suggestively closer and lowered his head. She could feel the warmth of his breath against her lips. He smelled delightful: fresh, spicy, and masculine. Automatically her eyes closed, and tingles shot through her body. He was going to kiss her, she realized, and an excitement she hadn't felt in years took hold of her. One of his arms slid around her shoulders as he closed the distance between them.

"Not burned," he murmured, his lips almost touching hers. "Singed a little, maybe. Heated, melted, fired up—"

"Daniel!" Shaken, she jerked her face away before his mouth could take hers. He was a total stranger, and a dangerous one at that. "I don't even know you."

"You will," he promised. He withdrew the threatened kiss and pulled her easily in the direction of the car. "Let's go."

His hand remained locked on her arm as they walked to the Porsche. The night air was crisp and cold, and the frozen snow crunching beneath their feet sparkled crystalline in the light from the old-fashioned streetlamps.

Daniel handed her into the sporty car, and she stretched in the luxury of the soft leather seat. Nice, she thought as he went around and let himself into the driver's seat.

Graham's car was a clattery old Chevy.

"I can imagine a worse fate," she said as he put the car in gear and glided away from the curb. "I can see the headlines now: Wealthy Fraud-Exposer Bewitches Gypsy Fortune-Teller; She prefers Porsche to broomstick."

He gave her one of his more endearing smiles. "Where do you live?"

"In Salem, of course. Where else?"

"You're kidding."

"Yes," she laughed, pulling off her scarf and shaking her long dark hair free. Daniel glanced sideways and stared at it; she could feel the touch of his eyes. "Across the river, in Cambridge. I have a small house near Radcliffe. Do you know Cambridge?"

"Intimately."

It was not in front of her small house that Daniel Haggarty stopped his car ten minutes later, however; he parked at a local Greek-Arabic restaurant in North Cambridge that was famous for its festive atmosphere and its belly dancers.

"I'm starving," he told her. "There was hardly any food at that party."

"It's almost midnight. You want to eat at midnight?"

"I suppose you're on a perpetual diet, like all the other other women I know?"

For some reason she resented this reference to "all the other women." She imagined them lining up, waiting their turn in his bedroom. "No, as a matter of fact, I'm not on a diet, and I adore Arabic food, even at midnight." And she was out the door before he could get around to open it for her.

The restaurant was crowded despite the late hour, and people were getting up and dancing to the exotic twang of the Middle Eastern music provided by tabor drums, a violin, and an oud. Bret and Daniel sat in a dark corner across from the band, at a tiny table for two. He apologized when his long legs bumped hers under the table, but he didn't move them.

"What do you want? A full-course meal?" she asked him.

"How about a couple of appetizers and some wine?"

"Terrific. Baba ghanouj and homos."

"They're full of garlic," he warned.

"I don't mind if you don't."

His mouth curled suggestively. "Isn't garlic supposed to ward off evil spirits? I'll eat it to fortify myself."

"I'm a witch, Daniel, not a vampire."

He launched directly into a Dracula impression. "But you vill be, daaarlink, ven I suck the blood from your sveet little neck." His eyes sought the spot, and Bret felt her pulse scampering there, as fast and uneven as static.

"It's wine you're going to drink tonight, Drac," she retorted, lifting the menu. "How about some retsina?"

"Clever. You read my mind."

"Most people don't care for retsina. They say it has an odd taste." She screwed up her nose and laughed at him. "I love it."

Daniel reached across the table and grasped her hand. "Bret" was all he said, but a dozen other messages came through, heating her flesh and softening her bones. She suddenly understood why he'd brought her to the restaurant. He was hungry for more than just food, but the time in the car together hadn't been long enough for him to ensure that she wouldn't simply slam her front door in his face. He wanted to get to know her a little better so it wouldn't seem so abrupt when he made his move.

She was about to tell him straightforwardly that he might as well forget it—that attractive though she found him, she simply didn't jump into bed with men she had known only a couple of hours. That she didn't jump into bed with men, period. That there had been no one since Arthur died.

But before she could say anything, the waiter appeared

at their side, and Daniel dropped her hand to order. Moments later the band launched into a loud, rhythmic pounding as a voluptuous belly dancer made her appearance in the dark smoke-filled room. "Ah, I like this part," said Daniel, shifting his gaze to the vision in crimson and gold veils and sequins who danced out among them, tinkling her tiny brass zils between her fingertips.

"Great for the stomach muscles," Bret observed caustically.

There were two more belly dancers before the retsina was drunk and the spicy appetizers consumed. There was also a pleasant exchange of easy, companionable conversation. Daniel was charming, witty, and intelligent, Bret discovered. And in spite of his hostility toward her supposed profession, he gave every indication of being just as pleased with her as she was with him.

"So why do you hate all the myriad practitioners of the occult?" she finally got up the nerve to ask.

"I told you: because you cheat people and prey on their superstitions."

"Not all psychics are frauds," she protested. "Some have genuine powers."

He snorted into his retsina.

"No, really. Don't you at least believe in ESP?" She was dabbing up the last of the homos with a bit of pita bread, making sure she got every last bit of the tasty dip out of the dish. Daniel watched her with a smile, obviously enjoying her hearty appetite.

"Surely you don't think science has solved all the riddles of the workings of the human brain?" she added, licking her lips.

"No," he admitted. His eyes were on her mouth, and his voice sounded abstracted. He cleared his throat. "There are still a few mysteries, but I'm confident that sooner or later they'll all be logically cleared up. Some 'practitioners of the occult' are just a helluva lot cleverer than others."

"So you claim to be a strict rationalist? What I saw in your hand denies that."

"Don't start with that palmistry garbage again. I only let you do it because I wanted the pleasure of your fingers on my palm."

She flushed, remembering that pleasure. He moved one hand across the table, threatening to repeat it. When she folded both her hands in her lap, he laughed at her and changed the subject.

They proved to have a lot of interests in common: books, political opinions, even sports. "You cross-country ski?" she cried. "I love to cross-country ski. But I haven't done it in years!" Arthur hadn't been particularly athletic, she recalled sadly.

"Whoever heard of a witch on skis?" he teased.

She decided to attack *his* profession for a change. "How come you're not on TV yourself, Haggarty?" she demanded. "Especially if you're as sexy and good-looking as you claim to be? I'll bet it would give the ratings a boost if you roasted your victims yourself instead of making your underlings do it."

"Maybe I'll take you up on that," he said complacently. "The day I do a segment on you."

A few glasses of retsina had made her reckless. "Any time, Daniel," she said cheerfully. "Why don't you forget about my mother and put me on your show? It would do wonders for my career. Believe me, I can use all the publicity I can get."

"You don't know what you're talking about." His voice was sharp. "Publicity like that could destroy your career."

"Really?" She grinned innocently at him. It had been on the tip of her tongue several times to tell him the truth about her career, but he was so smug on the subject that she simply couldn't take pity on him yet. "Then I suppose I should be afraid of you, shouldn't I? But, Daniel, you seem so nice."

He scowled. She could tell he was having second thoughts about "burning" her, a fact that gave her immense satisfaction.

By the time the last belly dancer of the evening performed, Bret had relaxed completely. She was clapping and swaying her own body to the sensuous music. "I love it! I think I'm going to take exotic dance lessons myself."

Daniel hadn't been watching the belly dancer for some time. His eyes were fixed on Bret's green silk blouse. "Tell me when. I'll be happy to poke dollar bills into your cleavage."

"Dollar bills! Is that all? How about hundreds?"

He met her mischievous gaze. "You already know I think you're worth at least that," he said warmly. His glance darted briefly toward "Zenobia," then returned to Bret. "You're a much higher class witch than she is." He signaled the waiter that he wanted the check. "Shall we go?"

Bret's smile vanished abruptly. Go where? Home, to her house, to her bed? A higher class witch. Why did she have the feeling that the word *witch* was synonymous with *whore*? She remembered some of his earlier remarks, and she suddenly wondered what she was doing here, at one o'clock in the morning, laughing merrily with a blackhearted stranger who probably saw her as an easy conquest.

Bret knew from her wretched experiences with the two or three men she had dated since her husband's death that she gave the impression of being more free-spirited than she actually was. Her instinctive manner with people was warm and friendly, and she enjoyed a true zest for life. So far this evening she'd joked around with Daniel, and—she might as well admit it—flirted with him, too. But that was as far as it was going to go.

If, like the other men she'd dated, he saw her engaging behavior as a come-on, she'd better set him straight right here in the restaurant. Otherwise the evening would probably end in a tussle on her front porch.

"I'm not going to sleep with you, you know," she announced.

His eyes widened slightly. "Reading my mind again?" he drawled.

She grabbed her purse and extracted her wallet. "And I insist on paying for my half," she said firmly, dropping a ten-dollar bill on the saucer the waiter presented.

Daniel was unexpectedly emotional, glaring at her money as if it had insulted him. "I hate this. If I pay, I'm a sexist; if I let you pay, I'm unchivalrous."

"The latter shouldn't be any problem, since you haven't even attempted chivalry so far," she said tartly.

His mouth thinned in a smile. "You're afraid if I pay for your supper, I'll demand your lovely body in return?"

"Look, Daniel, let's not complicate things, okay? I've enjoyed this evening—I don't get out very often—and I've even enjoyed, well, sparring with you. But that's as far as it goes. I don't sleep with men."

There was a brittle silence before Daniel asked, "Who do you sleep with?"

She realized what he was thinking and smothered a laugh. "I don't sleep with anybody," she explained. "Well, except Chester. My cat."

"You sleep with a *cat?*"

"Not always. I try to kick him out, but sometimes the monster waits till I'm asleep, then crawls under the covers beside me."

"Dear God, the witch keeps a cat," Daniel growled. "I'm allergic to cats. Whenever I'm in the same room with one I start sneezing with all the force of an erupting volcano."

"That settles it," she said with a sigh of mock relief. "You'll have a hard time making unscrupulous advances if you're busy sneezing."

"Don't count on it. I'll take an antihistamine."

On that note he rose and led her out to get their coats.

Sitting beside him in the dark car, she watched his hands moving on the gearshift and the steering wheel. He was wearing thin leather driving gloves—black, like the rest of his attire. She had a brief mental image of his gloved hands sliding over her naked flesh. Idiot, she chided herself. Save the fantasies for when you're alone, safely locked away from this very exciting and dangerous man.

They didn't speak except to give and acknowledge the directions to her house, which was located on a quiet residential street two blocks from the noise and traffic of Cambridge's Massachusetts Avenue. When he pulled up under the huge elm in front of her house, she opened her mouth to say good night, but he was out of the car and around to her side before she could get the words out.

"You don't have to see me to the door," she protested as he leaned down to help her.

He didn't even bother to argue. He simply took her arm and marched her up the walk to the front porch of the turn-of-the-century house. He hovered over her while she fumbled for her keys, and she nervously wondered whether he was going to try to push past her into the house. Forcible entry was the only way he'd get in, she had firmly decided. Daniel Haggarty was definitely not the sort of man you could offer a cognac to and then dismiss.

She found the key and inserted it, then quickly turned to him with her back against the door. "Thank you for a pleasant . . ." she began, but her words died as she was trapped in the smoldering blaze of his hypnotic eyes. He was standing very close, and while she waited helplessly, her fingers clenched around the keys, he moved closer still, pressing her against the solid oak door. She gasped as she realized that the first contact between them was not to be a kiss at all, but the exciting surge of his already aroused body against her own.

His dark coat was open down the front, and hers seemed to offer her little protection against the elemental masculine challenge in him. "Daniel," she protested weakly as he moved against her in a way that made her ache with desire.

His forehead touched hers; his gloved hands speared into her hair and cradled her head. His lips were very near hers as he whispered, "I'm sorry, Bret. I don't mean to be offensive. I just want you to know how much I need you, how much I've burned for you all evening. I've never felt like this, acted like this. Don't be angry."

"I'm not," she whispered back, wondering why she wasn't.

"You're so warm, so sweet, so full of life," he murmured. His tongue touched her lips, stroking lightly over the sensitive contours, probing the corners provocatively. She shuddered and slipped her arms around his neck. Colors were flashing in front of her eyes again in bright, triumphant, rainbow bursts. She, too, was burning.

His hands urged her face closer. His kiss was gentle. At first his lips did nothing more than mold hers, seeming to try their shape, enjoy their taste. He sucked and nibbled and drew back, leaving her so bereft that she exerted pressure with her hands on the back of his neck to bring their mouths together again. She felt him sigh and heard him mutter something unintelligible in the instant before his control evaporated and his kiss turned fiercely demanding.

Bret pressed her body to his as his tongue drove into her mouth, exploring every inch with its rapid, sinuous delving, darting against her teeth, engaging her own tongue in loving battle as she tried some exploration of her own. Her mouth opened fully to him as a knot tightened in the pit of her stomach. It was a soul-wrenching kiss, a sorcerer's kiss, a kiss that both asked for and promised satisfaction.

"You're wonderful, sweetheart," he exclaimed, jerking his head back for an instant. "I can't remember when I've ever been so turned on by a kiss." One of his leather-encased fingers slid down over her face, touched her lips, then moved to the pounding pulse in her throat. He dropped two teasing, feather-light kisses on her tingling lips. "Invite me in," he ordered softly.

"No, Daniel, I can't," she whispered, wishing desperately that she could.

"You can." His mouth took the place of his finger on her throat, and she felt the exquisite sensation of his tongue chafing her skin while her blood beat just beneath it. Liquid warmth blossomed in her, and there were spasms all through her, everywhere. He let her feel a hint of teeth. "Let me in," he urged in his Dracula accent. "Let me teach you all manner of dark, sensual delights."

She giggled delightedly. Surely a man who could joke at a time like this couldn't be all that much of a threat. "Sorry, Drac, but I'm not that foolish. The vampire has to be invited in the first time, but after that he can enter at will."

"Hmm. I'll remember that," he swore, raising his lips to seize her mouth in an unchecked, passionate attack that was duplicated by the erotic rocking of his hips. She could feel the sensual tension in his hard-muscled body, and she quickly reevaluated the situation. He was a threat, all right. How could she have forgotten, even for a fraction of a second, the danger she had sensed in him from the first moment she laid eyes on him?

She suddenly remembered Graham's words: "A yielding little fish like you could easily be swallowed up and crushed." No. She wasn't yielding, and she was not about to be crushed!

With difficulty she freed her lips. "No more, Daniel, please. I'm sorry. I did warn you."

Anger flashed in his eyes for only an instant before rueful acceptance took its place. He expelled his breath heavily, and she could feel his arms trembling. "You warned me," he admitted. "You don't sleep with men you've just met."

"I don't sleep with men at all."

"I don't believe that. You're beautiful, sexy, and there's not a hint of coldness about you." His dark eyes turned speculative. "There's someone else?"

"No. There's no one else. I just don't want an affair at present. I'm too busy enjoying my independence."

"You're attracted to me," he pointed out, moving provocatively against her once again, making her insides melt.

"Stop it." This time she twisted away, half turning toward the door. "I'm freezing, and I'm going inside. Good night, Daniel."

"Wait. Can't we thrash this out a little more? I'm willing to talk about our options, Bret."

"It's nearly two in the morning! I'm too exhausted to talk any more tonight. I have to get up and swim tomorrow morning."

"In the middle of winter?"

"I swim for exercise at the Cambridge Fitness Club every morning," she explained patiently. "If I miss it, I feel lousy all day."

"I like a woman who keeps in shape," he said huskily, brushing his lips against hers. "Kiss me again."

The temptation to do so was almost too great to resist. But she knew she must resist. She had just started, very tentatively, to date again. She knew she wasn't ready for a sexual adventure with a man as devastatingly attractive as Daniel. She wouldn't be able to handle it. "No, Daniel! You may be attracted to me, but don't forget that you disapprove of my, uh, profession. I certainly haven't forgotten your threats."

The reminder made his jaw tighten, and once more there was a flash of hostility in his eyes. "You've made *me* forget," he admitted. "I think you *are* a witch."

This annoyed her. "You desire me, so I'm a witch? You *do* sound like a Puritan!"

He took a step back and thrust his hands deep into the pockets of his coat. "I was under the impression that the attraction between us was mutual."

Her gaze dropped beneath his relentless stare. "I'd be an idiot to be attracted to a man who's already declared his intention to burn me."

"It was just a metaphor, for heaven's sake."

"Yes, but its connotations are cruel."

"I'm not going to hurt you, Bret." He moved closer to her again, but he kept his hands in his pockets, as if to prove his good faith. "When can I see you again?"

"Daniel, I really don't think—"

"When?" His voice was peremptory, harsh. "Tomorrow night? For dinner?"

"So we can have this same argument all over again? No, Daniel. I'm not going to get involved with you."

"You are." He pulled his gloved hands from his pockets and held her face softly. "You've no free will in this matter, Bret Kingsley. I'm your fate, and you're mine." He kissed her again, far more tenderly than she'd expected, stealing her breath, bewitching her body. Then he drew back, ran his hands through her silky black hair, and turned to leave.

When he reached his car he stopped and looked back. "Go inside," he ordered. "I won't leave until I know you're safely ensconced in your fortress."

Whoever said he was unchivalrous? Bret bit her lip, wishing with all her heart that it could have been different, wishing she had the courage, the freedom, the easygoing attitude about sex that most women her age seemed to possess. "Good-bye," she said as she opened the door.

"Never say good-bye," he answered, lounging in all his masculine glory against the side of his car. "The chase is just beginning."

Chapter

3

THE CHASE, BRET thought in exasperation as the telephone rang at midnight toward the end of the following week, was gradually wearing her down. D. D. Haggarty was nothing if not persistent. He called her at least once every day, usually at night before she went to bed. Once he even sent her a box of chocolates, which she devoured even as she complained to him that night on the phone that he was ruining her figure. But she continued to refuse his requests for a date.

He wasn't giving up though. No matter how many times she told him to forget it, he always came back with another suggestion: dinner, cocktails, a movie, the symphony, an exhibition at the Museum of Fine Arts, and so on. Sooner or later, he said, he was going to find some activity that would tempt her.

"Hello, Daniel," she said that night as she lifted the telephone. "Doesn't it ever worry you that I might be asleep at this hour?"

"Bret?" said a puzzled female voice on the other end. Oh, Lord! "Mother?"

"Who's Daniel?" demanded Iris Carter. "Is there a new man in your life, my dear?"

In this respect, at least, Bret reflected wryly, her mother was as normal as anybody else's. Her patience with her daughter's widowhood had begun to wear thin.

"The time is ripe for you to fall in love," Iris went on blithely. "In fact, it could well explain the slight difference in your aura that I commented on when you came over last Sunday. There was a distinct rose-colored glow."

"Good heavens, Mum." Bret sighed. "You and your auras. I don't intend to see the man again, much less fall in love with him." She drew a quick breath and tried to change the subject. Once her mother got started on her daughter's love life, she was liable to go on about it all night. "Are you all right? Why are you calling so late?"

"Oh, is it late? I didn't notice. I was having a long talk with Angelique, and when she mentioned her daughter I remembered there was something I wanted to ask you about. What was it now? Poor Angelique is having such trouble with that child of hers, you know."

"Hmm," Bret replied, knowing better than to ask for details, particularly since Angelique was an eighteenth-century French ghost. Bret vaguely remembered that she'd been guillotined in the Reign of Terror.

"Something about television," Iris went on. "Poor Angelique didn't know what I was talking about, of course. A box where you can see people walking about and speaking as if in life. What is the world coming to, she wanted to know. She absolutely couldn't understand when I told her that I was actually going to *be* on television. She was concerned that it might affect my health."

Bret snapped to attention. "What do you mean, you're going to be on television?"

"Why, darling, I had the most fascinating conversation today with such a nice man who wants to do a TV program about my 'illustrious career,' as he put it. Can you imagine? And I was convinced everybody had forgotten all about me."

"You didn't agree, I hope?" Bret said on a rising note of panic.

"There, Bret, you sound so concerned. I appreciate it, but you really mustn't be so protective."

"Was this 'nice man' named D. D. Haggarty by any chance?"

"Why, yes. Mr. Haggarty, I believe. But by the end of the conversation he was telling me to call him Daniel." There was an intake of breath, and Bret could practically feel her mother's intuitive powers flashing along the phone wire. She might be flaky, but she wasn't thick. "Your Daniel?"

"He's not my Daniel," Bret said grimly. "He's the TV producer responsible for a local show called *Facts and Fantasy*, and he's a very dangerous man. Not to mention unscrupulous. I can't believe he actually called you up and pretended to be pleasant! He hates spiritualists."

"Really?" Iris sounded a bit disconcerted. "And I'm usually such a good judge of character."

That, thought Bret, was a laugh and a half. Her mother could look into a person's palm and read every nuance of his or her personality, but no matter how reprehensible the faults she uncovered, she seemed to forget about them the moment she dropped the subject's hand. "I look for the good in people," she had frequently told her daughter. "Never once have I failed to find it."

As a result, Iris Carter was routinely cheated by everyone from car mechanics to financial advisers.

"What did you agree to?" Bret demanded.

"Well, nothing yet. I explained to him that although I was very flattered by the invitation to appear on his program, I'd have to discuss it with my daughter first."

Bret breathed a sigh of relief. "Thank goodness, Mum. I'll talk to him and convey your regrets. He'll simply have to understand that you're retired and don't do interviews anymore." Her voice tightened as she added, "I'll make sure he doesn't bother you again."

"But Bret—"

"No buts. Do you remember your old friend Myra Kelley?"

"Of course. A pleasant woman, and quite talented," Iris said a little uncertainly.

"She was a fake, Mum, and you know it. One of Haggarty's interviewers exposed her on the show a couple of months ago. They reduced her to tears and blasted what was left of her credibility. That was only the beginning as far as Daniel is concerned. He doesn't believe in supernatural phenomena, and he means to prove that all psychics are either charlatans or kooks."

"Good heavens!" Her mother was clearly shocked. "And he sounded like such a charming young man on the phone."

"He's charming all right," Bret said grimly, remembering the way he had nearly seduced her. "He'd charm the fish out of the sea and then grill them over an open fire."

It wasn't until she'd hung up that she remembered her birth sign and Daniel's threats, and she shivered at the aptness of her metaphor.

The next morning, Saturday, Bret stepped out of her swim club into the chill of a dreary February wind to find Daniel leaning against his Porsche, waiting for her. He was casually dressed in blue jeans and a black bomber jacket, and his hair was agreeably ruffled by the wind. He looked rough and tough and sexy as hell.

Bret frowned as he came up to her and took her gym bag out of her hands. "What are you doing here?"

"Good morning to you, too," his amused voice returned. "Are you always so pleasant at this ungodly hour?"

She glanced at her watch. It was nine o'clock. "It's not *that* ungodly. I usually swim at six."

"Spare me," he groaned.

"Go away, Daniel. I don't want to have anything more to do with you."

He merely grinned, looking pleased with himself. "No, Bret. You've been doing your best to avoid me, but I've stalked you down now, and I intend to take you out to breakfast. After all that exercise you must be starving."

"Breakfast!"

"You keep turning down my invitations to assorted evening activities," he pointed out.

"I work in the evenings."

"Ah, yes." As always, his voice turned severe at the reminder of her work. "I keep forgetting—night is the best time for casting spells."

A puckish grin came over Bret's face. In her concern over her mother, she'd forgotten that D. D. Haggarty still persisted in thinking of Bret Kingsley as a professional psychic. It was remarkable, under the circumstances, that he continued to demonstrate such an interest in her. He seemed to take some sort of perverse pleasure in pursuing a woman of whom he thoroughly disapproved.

"Breakfast, huh?" Now that he mentioned it, her stomach was growling. The clever devil really knew how to prey on her weaknesses. First the chocolates, now this. "Can we have pancakes?"

"I was thinking of something sophisticated and continental, like croissants and light, fluffy omelets."

"Blueberry pancakes," she said decisively. "With maple syrup and great dollops of butter."

"With a side of bacon and a side of hash browns, and a bottomless pot of coffee," he added, obviously warming to the prospects.

"Sounds divine. There's a pancake place in the Square, just a few minutes from here."

"The Square," he said with a sigh. "Okay, but it's up to you to find me a place to park."

Thirty minutes later, after three fruitless tours of Harvard Square, Daniel finally shelled out for a parking place in an expensive underground garage, muttering darkly about the problems of owning a car in the city, and led his captive into the local Pancake Heaven. Sitting down opposite him, Bret felt the heat of his charcoal eyes. As it had before, his gaze seemed to touch her with fire. But she didn't let that stop her from digging into a huge helping of blueberry pancakes splathered with maple syrup.

"One of my favorite things about you is the obvious pleasure you take in appeasing your appetite," he said with a wicked grin. "Do you gratify your other desires with the same enthusiasm?"

"What other desires?" she asked innocently. "Good food, in my opinion, is the only pleasure that counts."

"I could introduce you to some others."

"I knew you were going to say that." She took a slow swallow of coffee and smiled at him. He looked a little less dangerous by day than he had by night. His complexion was not as dark as she'd thought. In fact, his skin was quite fair against his dark hair and eyes. He'd taken off the black leather jacket, revealing a perfectly respectable white cable-knit sweater. All in all, he looked a good deal less satanic than she remembered.

"And?" he prompted.

"And the answer is still no."

To her surprise, he didn't pursue it. Instead, he said, "How can you eat so much and still stay so thin?"

"I'm not thin!"

"Slender, then," he corrected himself, letting his eyes roam over her. She, too, was dressed casually this morning in a blue V-necked sweater, jeans, crimson leg-warmers, and soft leather boots. Her black hair, which was still damp from the pool, was loosely tied back with a blue ribbon.

"I work out. Swimming, running, lifting weights."

"Lifting weights?"

"Sure. Lots of women do it, particularly in my line of work." Indeed, she didn't know a single actor or actress who didn't work like hell to keep in shape.

But Daniel misinterpreted. "You have to be strong, I suppose, to tip tables at seances without getting caught. Everything I've researched about the history of spiritualism suggests that mediums have always been athletic. Some of them were even able to perform remarkable feats of contortionism."

Bret raised her eyes at the ceiling in a here-we-go-again gesture.

"There was a famous nineteenth-century medium who used to have herself bound with cords around the neck, waist, wrists, and ankles in her cabinet before every performance. This was supposed to insure that the figure who materialized from the cabinet after the medium went into her trance was really a spirit entity and not the medium herself in a disguise. The bindings were always double-checked to make sure she couldn't possibly free herself."

"But she could free herself, I take it?"

"Let's put it this way: The spirit's features were extraordinarily similar to the medium's, and the two of them were never seen together." He took a swallow of coffee, and his eyes glinted at her over the rim of his cup as he added, "Did your mother teach you that particular trick, Bret? Shall I take you home and tie you up and see whether you can get free?"

Bret nearly choked on her pancakes. His voice was so starkly sensual that it made heat wash through her like a wave. She clutched her fork tightly for a moment, then put it down carefully on the side of her plate. This had to stop!

"Look, Daniel, I don't know how to get it through to you that I'm not interested in the lurid affair you're apparently offering. You don't even like or approve of me, and there's no way I'm going to get mixed up with a man who regards me as an object of—of derision."

His hand reached out and folded over hers. She shivered. Why was it that she was so damnably susceptible to his slightest touch?

"Forgive me if I've given you that impression," he said. "I like you very much."

"I'm not sure I believe you. I think you're just after me for sex." She slid her hand out from under his.

"Come on," he said a little impatiently. "If sex were all I wanted, I could get it elsewhere, believe me."

She did. With his looks, his charm, and his confidence, no doubt he'd been getting it regularly since puberty.

"What do you want then?"

"A chance," he said simply.

"A chance for what?"

He held up his hand, palm toward her. "A chance to channel my energy into the one deep line that comes after the ragged false starts."

She stared at him in shock. "I thought you didn't believe in palmistry."

"As a science I don't. As a way of looking at one's life, though, it's rather intriguing." His eyes were completely serious for once. "I'm thirty-six, Bret, and for nearly five years I've been divorced from a wife who left me to 'find herself.' I'm disenchanted with the swinging-singles routine. I'd like to get to know someone on a deeper, less superficial level, and I sense that possibility between us. Don't you?"

She frowned, thinking about it. Every night that week, as she lay curled up in her lonely bed trying to sleep, she'd been fantasizing about him. She'd remembered the warmth of his mouth on hers, the exciting hardness of his body. She fell asleep each night imagining that he was with her in bed, pressing her down with his weight and loving her all over.

Sex. Yes, she could imagine that with him. But anything more? He was so different from Arthur—much more domineering, much more dynamic. His charisma certainly added an extra charge to the sensual attraction between them, but there was so much more to a relationship than that. Life had been sunny and tranquil with Arthur; with Daniel it would be turbulent and maybe even dark.

"Well?" he demanded. "What are you thinking?"

She stopped brooding and ate the last mouthful of pancakes. "I don't know, Daniel. I find you a very disruptive influence at a time in my life when I don't think I'm ready for any disruptions. I'm a little frightened of you, if you want to know the truth."

He frowned, but she sensed he wasn't entirely displeased by her admission. He probably enjoyed frightening people!

"Are you afraid I might make good my threat to include you in my program on psychic fraud?" he inquired, his dark eyes gleaming.

"Oh, dear God, no," she laughed. "Daniel, really, I think we ought to clear that up before—"

"Or your mother? You're afraid for your mother—is that it? Do you think I'm trying to get close to you in hopes of prying all sorts of anecdotes out of you about one of the best-known mediums in the country?"

She glared at him over the rim of the coffee cup she had lifted to her lips. "The possibility has occurred to me, yes. Especially after that stunt you pulled yesterday when you called her and tried to charm her into an interview."

"You heard about that, huh?" He didn't sound overly concerned.

"Naturally I heard about it. My mother and I are very close. The answer is no, by the way. She doesn't do interviews."

His eyelids flickered. "But I've got you, and you probably know all her tricks of the trade. No doubt you could be persuaded to provide me with the intriguing details of how she rigs the room before a seance."

"Is that what you really want from me?" she cried. The coffee cup slammed down onto its saucer. "Well, you're out of luck, Haggarty! Even if I possessed any such knowledge—which I don't, because my mother's not a fake—there's no way I would ever 'be persuaded' to divulge it to you!"

"Of course she's a fake," Daniel said in a voice that was low but intense. "And I do mean to interview her, you know. I want to be completely honest with you on that score. I despise spiritualists. No matter what happens between you and me, I intend to go ahead with my efforts to discredit them all."

"Nothing's going to happen between you and me. I've already told you, you're too narrow-minded and judgmental for me." She paused, then added, "My mother's an old lady, Daniel, and she's always been a little cracked. She's living in retirement now, she's not very healthy, and she's not doing seances. I hardly think she's an appropriate target for one of your attacks."

He shrugged, but his eyes were hard. He was a complex personality, she thought: hot and cold, harsh and gentle, driven in his professional pursuits and heaven only knew what in his personal life. She couldn't resist comparing him once again to Arthur, who had been even-tempered and genuinely kind. Kindness, especially, was a virtue Bret valued highly. There was too much cruelty, too much aggression in the world. She didn't want to get mixed up with a man whose professional goals demanded that he ruthlessly hunt down a harmless sixty-five-year-old woman and expose her in the public stocks of prime-time television.

"I have to go," she said. She thrust her hand into her pocketbook and pulled out her wallet. Before she got it open, his hand came down over hers.

"Not this time, witch. I suggested this, and I'm paying. As for your mother, forget about her. All I really care about is you. I want you, and I'm not letting you walk out of my life."

The steel underlying his words both chilled and excited her. Dear heavens, the man was a menace! She put her wallet away. *Let* him pay, dammit.

"I'm sorry, but I'm leaving."

He rose when she did. "I'm coming with you."

"You can't."

"Stop me."

She thrust her arms into her crimson fleeced-lined jacket and tied her white wool scarf around her neck, then turned to stalk toward the door. Daniel put on his own jacket and followed, taking a firm grip on her upper arm.

"Are you going to make a scene in a public restaurant?" she hissed.

"You're the one making the scene. I'm being a perfect gentleman. Watch, I'll demonstrate." He made a show of holding the door open for her and bowing obsequiously as she stepped out into the street. "Forgive me. I've made the lady mad," he added in an exaggeratedly humble tone.

She caught the teasing look in his eyes and found herself stifling a smile. Devil, she thought. Arrogance she could resist, but his unpredictable bursts of humor left her defenseless.

"I've already told you, Bret, I won't do anything to

hurt you." He paused, then added, his rueful tone testifying to the cost of his concession, "Or your mother, either, if she's really as old and feeble as you say she is."

Bret reflected guiltily that her mother *wasn't* as old and feeble as she'd intimated, but she kept that thought to herself. The February wind made her shiver as it whistled around the buildings in Harvard Square. Daniel's arm came around her shoulders, drawing her close to his warm, hard body. "I promise I won't interview her without your permission . . . or hers."

She tried to shrug free, unsure whether or not she could trust him, but he held her tightly. "Relax," he murmured, his breath hot against her ear. "You're as slippery as a fish."

And as easily hooked, she thought sadly. "I am a fish. A Pisces."

He made a face. "Don't tell me you're into astrology as well?"

His easy, amused tone disarmed what was left of her resistance, and she began to think she'd been precipitous in her desire to escape. He couldn't be as ruthless as she'd thought if he was really willing to leave her mother alone.

Taking a deep breath of the fresh, cold air, she allowed him to walk her back toward the underground garage. She might as well let him drive her home. It was much too cold to stand outside waiting for a bus. Besides, she'd left her gym bag in his car.

"We psychics are all into astrology," she said archly. "When's your birthday, Daniel?"

"I'm not going to tell you."

"Why not?"

"You'll say we're incompatible and use it as an excuse to keep up this stubborn coyness of yours."

"Graham has you pegged as a Scorpio. Were you born in November?"

"No. So much for Graham's wisdom."

"That's too bad. Pisces and Scorpio are among the most compatible lovers in the zodiac."

He brightened immediately. "If I were a Scorpio, would you make love with me?"

Since he wasn't born in November, she shrugged and risked a light answer. "I might consider it. Graham says the sex would be terrific."

They had reached the entrance to the garage. It got dark as they descended the stairs to the lower level, and Bret was conscious of the increasing pressure of Daniel's arm around her. "I'm a Scorpio," he announced.

"I don't believe you. When's your birthday?"

"You're going to laugh," he predicted.

"Tell me."

"I was born on your favorite day of the year," he said mysteriously.

"What does that mean?"

He maintained a mock stubborn silence as they walked through the quiet garage toward the car, but he finally gave in and answered, "October thirty-first, witch."

She did laugh, delightedly. Then she stopped, because they had reached the car and he was forcing her up against it and kissing her fiercely. Their bodies melted together, and fire leaped through her. "You *are* a Scorpio," she murmured against his lips.

"And the sex will be terrific," he agreed.

His gloved hands threaded through her hair and held her motionless while his mouth played teasingly on hers. She gasped as his tongue wet the surface of her lips, then traced tiny patterns over her cheeks and eyelids. The damp butterfly kisses were deliciously erotic, and she was passive for only a few moments before her fingers slipped into his hair and pulled his mouth back to hers.

"Mmm," he groaned deep in his throat. Their tongues touched, and Bret's limbs grew heavy with desire. She pressed closer, crushing her breasts against his chest.

Their jackets impeded them, so they strained against each other, trying to feel through the barrier of cloth.

The kiss deepened. Bret trembled as his tongue ran along the edge of her teeth, teased her gums, then stroked her own tongue with devastating sensual expertise. Bursts of liquid warmth exploded in her, drugging her. His hands slid down her back and kneaded her bottom, forcing her lower body against his. He felt wonderful. He was obviously aroused, and this knowledge thrilled her, making her arch herself against him in joyous celebration of her feminine power.

Her head tilted back as his kisses moved ravenously down her throat. She sighed, wanting him desperately, needing him. Her loins ached as she absorbed the pressure of his thighs against her own—pressure that made her limp and hot and dizzy and barely aware of who she was or what she was doing.

"Bret," he whispered, taking her name up in a breathless litany of "Bret, Bret, Bret." He sounded as incoherent as she was. His body trembled; his face was flushed and damp against her own. He slid them both sideways along the car until she was leaning against the hood; then his strong arms lifted her so she was sitting on it. She nuzzled his throat with her lips and teeth as he parted her legs and stood in close between her thighs. His arms reached around to support her back as he insinuated himself still more tightly against her. She moaned his name. Her legs curled around his waist, and she clung to him as if the world were coming to an end and he was going to be taken from her.

One of his hands jerked open her jacket and sought her breasts. His gloves made him clumsy, so he bent his head and tore them off with his teeth in a gesture that was savagely exciting. "Oh, Daniel," she breathed as his bare hand slid under her sweater, pushed her thin bra up, and took her warmth in his hot palm.

"I know, my darling, you feel so good." His fingertips

drew teasing circles around the peak of her captured breast, making her moan and shudder in his arms. His head came down, and he kissed her breasts through her sweater. Her nipples had turned to hard, burning points, and she thought she would die if he didn't take them in his mouth. She held his head against her while his thighs pressed rhythmically now, signaling his need and stoking hers to a fever pitch. She was spinning on waves of explosive sexuality, tossed on a storm of desire that was much more intense than anything in her experience.

She was tearing at his jacket, longing to touch his naked flesh as he was touching hers, when a sudden arc of light distracted her. The headlights of another car beamed down on their entwined figures as somebody entered the garage. Bret buried her face on Daniel's shoulder in a sudden rush of embarrassment and slid from the car hood to her feet, her body moving deliciously along Daniel's as she regained her balance.

"We're in a public garage, for godsake," she reminded him, gasping for breath.

He freed one arm and flung open the car door. "Get in," he ordered. "We'll go to my place."

Trembling, she obeyed, sitting down and fastening her seat belt in a daze of frustrated longing. Dear heavens, she thought as her mind sluggishly began working again. She'd never known such a fever of desire, ever, in her life. She had never felt anything even vaguely similar with Arthur.

Arthur. A strange sense of disloyalty stabbed her, cutting right through her desire. How could she feel such intense yearning for a man like Daniel when her sexual feelings for her gentle, kind husband had been, in comparison, tame? It didn't seem right somehow.

She'd been alone too long, she told herself. Her natural urges had been stifled by her grief, and now that the grief had finally receded, those urges were burgeoning forth, clamoring for expression, making her eager to snatch the pleasure this very exciting man was offering.

But how would she feel when her physical demands were met? She knew the answer to that already. Without love, without commitment, she'd feel empty, used.

"Oh, no," she moaned as the Porsche sped out of the garage and into the light of morning. She closed her eyes against the brightness. "I can't go with you, Daniel."

The car jerked as he shifted recklessly. "Don't say that, Bret." His voice was taut with warning. "No second thoughts; I won't tolerate it."

"Do you think it's any easier for me?" she cried, sitting upright in her seat and glaring at him. She was furious with him and even more furious with herself. "Women are as capable of gut-wrenching lust as men are, and the frustration hurts us just as much!"

"We're two mature adults, Bret. We're not committed elsewhere, and there's no reason on earth for you to condemn us both to frustration."

"There's one very good reason, Haggarty. I'm just not ready for an affair yet."

His hands were white-knuckled on the steering wheel. "Yet?" he repeated, zeroing in on the operative word. "What do you mean, 'yet'? You want me to wine you and dine you for a couple of weeks first? You can't accept the explosive chemistry between us until some decorous courting period has elapsed? Is that it?"

"No, that's not it!" she retorted.

"You won't even accept a normal sort of date with me."

"Just take me home, Daniel. To my house, I mean."

Instead, he slammed on the brakes and pulled the car over to the side of the road. Her entire body tensed as he turned to her, a grim look etched on his face. He noted her stiffness, and his charcoal eyes turned sardonic. "Relax. I'm not about to assault you. I can take no for an answer. I just hate to, dammit!"

She smiled faintly and relaxed against the seat. He

has a beautiful mouth, she thought involuntarily, staring at it. Desire twisted in her again.

Daniel took a deep breath and closed his eyes. Bret stared at his thick eyelashes, which were even denser than her own. His face was drawn with emotion, and she felt an unexpected tenderness for him, which made her heart beat unevenly again.

"You said yourself that I was a man of unruly passions," he reminded her, raising his lashes again. "You were right. You also said sex was very important to me. You were right about that, too." The look in his dark eyes intensified. "I've been tortured since I met you. I lie in bed at night, unable to sleep, tormented by fantasies. If I weren't so positive that witchcraft and voodoo and all the black arts were a crock of bull, I'd be certain you'd put a spell on me."

"Daniel, I—"

"Be quiet. I'm going to ask you one question, and I want a straight answer. What does it mean, you're not ready yet? Are you ever going to be ready? Just how serious were you when you told me last weekend that you don't sleep with men? Are you afraid of sex? What the hell is the matter with you?"

"That's five questions."

One hand cupped her chin, forcing her to face him. "Answer me, dammit."

"All right." She urged herself to be as honest as he was. "It's very simple, really. You're not the only one who lies awake at night and fantasizes. I find you extremely exciting, Daniel. I was attracted to you the instant I saw you, leaning up against the wall at that party and glowering at me."

There was a glint of satisfaction in his eyes. "Go on."

"The trouble is, I was very much in love with Arthur," she said in a small voice.

"Your husband?"

"Yes. He's the only lover I've ever had, Daniel, and

sex between us was always an act of love. I know it sounds ridiculous in this day and age, but I just can't leap into a casual sexual adventure with a man I don't know. In a way I wish I could. My life's been so empty since he died." She was mortified to hear the little sob that caught at her throat. She tried to swallow it, but it would not be repressed. The next thing she knew she was weeping, and Daniel was holding her tight against his chest, smoothing her hair tenderly and murmuring gentle, undemanding nothings in her ear.

A half hour later, after a brisk walk along the Charles River with Daniel companionably holding her hand, Bret sat beside him once again as he drove her home.

They had hardly spoken since her outburst, but their silence was one of sympathy and understanding, and Bret felt more at ease with him than she'd felt since they met. Her respect for him had increased a hundredfold, as had her affection. Daniel Haggarty was turning out to be a good deal kinder than she'd originally thought.

Maybe she should just go ahead and sleep with him. He hadn't said it, but the bitter truth was there, staring them in the face: Her idyllic relationship with Arthur Kingsley was over forever. She'd avoided sex for three long years, but it wasn't realistic to keep running away from her desires just because she didn't feel the same emotional bond with Daniel that she'd felt with Arthur. She hardly knew Daniel; the bond might grow between them.

On the other hand, it might not. She shivered, hugging herself.

"Cold?" asked Daniel, turning up the heat.

"Uh, no, not really."

"What are you thinking?"

"Nothing much."

He pursed his lips, looking strained again. A couple of moments passed before he cast her a glance and said, "I want to see you tonight, Bret. I'll make dinner for you—how about that? I'm quite a good cook, you know."

"I can't."

"Bret, I respect your feelings, and I understand your reservations. I can't promise you anything at this point; I'd be a liar if I said I could. I want you desperately, but I'll do my best not to coerce you into bed before you're ready. I'll do anything you want, in fact, except go away. So stop arguing. We're going to get to know each other, and we're going to start by being together tonight."

"But I can't, Daniel," she said with genuine regret. "I'm working tonight." She had dress rehearsals all afternoon and evening. The New Cambridge Repertory's production of *Macbeth* was opening the following weekend.

He took his eyes off the road to stare at her, then had to swerve to avoid a bus. He cursed violently. "What is it tonight—another charitable party? Crystal balls and martinis on the rocks?"

She shook her head. It was time to tell him, she decided. This nonsense had gone on long enough. "No, Daniel, it's far more sinister than that. Tonight I'm going to be dressed in black, leaning over a cauldron, prophesying and murmuring incantations of doom." She wagged her fingers at him like a spook. "'Double double, toil and trouble, fire burn and cauldron bubble—'" she intoned, then stopped abruptly. It was unlucky to quote from The Scottish Play, as the actors in her company called it. Productions of *Macbeth* had a reputation in the theater for being fraught with disaster, and citing a line from the play was every bit as hazardous as mentioning it by name.

"Very funny," said Daniel.

She tossed her hair back over her shoulder and grinned. "Oh, but I'm serious. A very important personage is coming to consult me and my colleagues tonight. We're going to predict great glories for him...and great disasters. We're going to tempt him by appealing to his overweening ambition."

She expected him to understand that she was teasing, but Daniel glared at her in outrage. "You're actually sitting there plotting what to say to some poor sucker? You're even more of a charlatan than I thought!"

A ripple of pure merriment went through her, and she had to look away to contain her laughter. It felt good after all the tears. "I'm not a charlatan. I promise you that every prediction I make for this man will come true—even the manner of his death."

"You're going to predict somebody's death?!"

"Take it easy," she said as he careened around a corner.

"That's really despicable, Bret. I can't believe you'd do such a thing."

"Come watch me," she challenged.

"What do you mean?"

"Just what I said." Her eyes were twinkling. Let him see for himself exactly what kind of witch she was. "Come watch me perform, act, practice my witchcraft, do my job. You said you wanted to get to know me better. Something about relating to me on a deeper, less superficial level?"

"I've seen you perform," he growled. "Once was enough. I don't like it, Bret. I don't even want to think about it."

"If you can't accept my professional life, I really don't see how you can expect to have any sort of relationship with me," she said reasonably. "Suppose we got serious. The next thing I knew you'd probably be insisting I quit work!"

"That's right, I would," he snapped. "Don't forget, I could blow your little act wide open, darling. And if I ever catch you predicting people's deaths, dammit, I won't hesitate to do so. Many people are extraordinarily subject to the power of suggestion. You could be condemning some poor sod to die from sheer terror."

"Don't worry, Haggarty. This particular client deserves it. He's terrorized quite a few people himself, and besides, he's an ambitious, power-seeking murderer."

Daniel pulled the car to a jolting stop in front of her house. "A murderer?" he repeated. "Where are you performing tonight—in the state prison?"

When she just grinned at him, he relaxed and leaned back in his seat. "Okay, witch. You're having a little joke, aren't you?"

"Sort of," she confessed.

"Sort of?"

She swung open the Porsche's door. "Come tonight, Daniel, and find out. One thirty-seven Liberty Square," she added, giving him the address of the theater. "Eight o'clock. Tell the guy at the door you're a friend of Bret's."

"Forget it, lady!"

"See you tonight." She laughed and jumped out of the car.

Chapter

4

"IS HE OUT THERE?" an uncharacteristically nervous Bret demanded of her fellow actor, Graham.

"If he is, he's sitting in the back. I couldn't see the guy," Graham answered. He was adjusting his doublet and hose for his role of Malcolm, the dispossessed heir to the throne of Scotland who prevails in the end of the play, after the death of the tyrant Macbeth. "These blasted tights are baggy," he complained. "How am I supposed to look dashing and heroic in this getup?"

"I think it's rather sexy."

"Yeah?" Looking pleased, he preened in front of the greenroom mirror, then glanced over at Bret. "You look pretty sexy yourself. I thought the three Weird Sisters were ugly old hags. How come you look young and beautiful and delicious enough to eat?"

"Paul agreed with me that the ugly old crone interpretation is a cliché. A witch should be lovely and feminine and powerful in her sexuality. That's what makes you men afraid of us after all."

"Rot. I think you're just trying to knock the socks off D. D. Haggarty, luv. And you will, too, if he sees you dressed like that."

Bret smoothed the front of her black Renaissance gown. It had a square, low-cut neckline, and scarlet laces held the bodice together. The silken skirt of the gown was slashed down the front to reveal a scarlet underskirt, the flowing sleeves similarly slashed to reveal a scarlet lining. Her midnight-black hair was loose about her shoulders and threaded with black and scarlet ribbons. The overall effect was dramatically sensual.

"He probably didn't come. He said he wouldn't. And it's snowing, so the roads are probably a mess."

"I doubt if a little snow would faze that crusader. Besides, he probably doesn't give much credence to weather reports. Don't you know that all weather predictors are frauds?"

Bret smiled a little, then burst into laughter. "I can't wait to see his face when he realizes I'm an actress and that it's Macbeth's death I'm predicting! You should have heard him this morning, Graham. He was appalled."

"I hope for your sake he can take a joke. He's not going to be too pleased when he finds out you've been taking him for a ride."

"Serves him right," she chuckled. "I told him at the start that I was an actress, but he paid no attention. He might be annoyed at first, but I can handle that." She reflected a moment, remembering both the sense of danger in Daniel and his underlying tenderness. "I hope."

Graham made a show of buckling his swordbelt. "You've got the hots for the guy, don't you?"

Bret tightened the laces of her bodice. "I'm trying my utmost not to get involved with him."

"Yeah? Tell me another."

"I mean it, Graham." She'd been thinking about the matter all day. Ever since Daniel had kissed her in the garage, dissolving them both into a state of intense sexual urgency, she'd been able to think of little else. "I'm a quiet-living widow. He's a sophisticated swinger, way out of my league. I'd be crazy to let anything happen between us."

"I'm glad you realize that," Graham said quietly. "I was afraid you might be getting in over your head. He's not your type, Bret."

Bret flashed him a look of annoyance. It was all right for her to tell herself that, but she didn't appreciate hearing it from Graham!

"I heard from a friend of a friend that what the D. D. really stands for is Dastardly Deceiver," Graham went on. "He's apparently left several brokenhearted women in his wake."

"You're just jealous."

Graham moved a step closer to her, his eyes running over her figure in the provocative manner he usually reserved for other women. "Perhaps so," he admitted. "You know how I feel about you, luv."

"I know you're my best friend," she retorted, unwilling to think of him in any other way. He occasionally teased her with sexual innuendos, but he had never made any serious attempt to alter the platonic nature of their friendship. Most of the time he behaved in a brotherly fashion toward her, and she was content to keep it that way. She'd never been physically attracted to Graham.

But he'd been her rock of salvation in the aftermath of Arthur's death, coaxing, threatening, and cajoling her into taking an interest in life again. She trusted him, she could talk to him, and, in all ways but one, she loved him.

"Stop rolling your eyes at me and let me finish getting ready," she said lightly. "We've got more important things to do than worry about my love life or lack of one. I have to open this play, you know."

As if on cue, a man's voice bellowed, "Kingsley! Where the hell are you, dammit?"

"Oh, jeez," she muttered as Paul Tiele, their director, stormed into the dressing room, smoking the inevitable cigarette and looking more than usually agitated.

"What is this, *Antony and Cleopatra?*" he mocked when he found Bret and Graham together. "We got a play to do, Kingsley, remember? The hundreds of dollars' worth of cloth you're draped in is supposed to be exhibited onstage, not back here for our resident Lothario to admire. Admirable though you may be."

"Thanks a lot."

Tiele, a thin, prematurely gray man in his early forties whose nervous energy and peremptory manner annoyed his actors just a little less than his brilliance and originality dazzled them, considered her for a moment in silence, then stalked over to her, blew smoke in her face, took the bodice of her dress in his two strong hands, and jerked it up an inch. "You're too sexy. You're supposed to be seducing Mac—" —he stopped just short of speaking the name—"the Scot with visions of power, but one look at you and he'll send his dreams of kingship straight to hell."

"I thought that was the way you wanted me to play it, Paul."

"It is, to a point. But I usually see you in jeans and a sweat shirt, Kingsley. You look different in that dress." He glanced at Graham. "What are you smirking at, Hamilton?" He gave Graham's costume a critical examination, too. "Nice legs. But your hose are baggy."

Bret coughed from the cigarette smoke and laughed at Graham as he cursed and once again attacked his costume.

Five minutes later they were ready to begin the rehearsal. Then Bret remembered. "Paul, wait. I almost forgot. I inadvertently quoted a couple of lines from the play today. I'd better do the exorcism first," she said, referring to the ritual needed to banish the malevolence attendant on her mistake and protect the actors and crew from possible dire consequences.

Tiele choked on his own smoke and groaned. "Good grief, Kingsley! You never quote from The Scottish Play, particularly not on dress rehearsal night! Are you deliberately courting disaster? Just because you're one of the Weird Sisters doesn't mean you can take liberties of that kind, dammit. If anything goes wrong, I'll hold you personally responsible!"

"Okay, Paul, okay. Take it easy. Nothing's going to go wrong."

Tiele was known for being the most superstitious member of the company, and Bret was well aware that he was none too comfortable about doing the play at all. It was considered the most unlucky play in the entire theatrical canon.

Paul Tiele knew the details of every disaster that had ever occurred during a production of *Macbeth*, and there were a lot of them. Olivier had almost been killed by a freak stage accident in 1937 when he played Macbeth at the Old Vic, and in one of Gielgud's productions three of the actors had died during the rehearsals and the run. Bret had heard these tales told over and over, along with many others. Tiele had never directed *Macbeth* before, and, quite simply, he was petrified.

The time-honored method of dealing with the fatal slip of either naming the play or quoting lines from it was to perform a simple, though somewhat odd, ceremony. Like all the other actors in the company, Bret knew the routine by heart. She went out of the room, knocked, reentered, turned around from left to right three times in a circle, then burst into the most vigorously obscene swear words she knew. Graham, who was watching, raised his eyebrows. "Is that the raunchiest you can get? Quiet-living widow, indeed!"

Bret was glad Daniel wasn't backstage to witness the ritual. Actors were probably even more superstitious than most spiritualists, she realized.

Shortly thereafter, the dress rehearsal began. As First Witch, Bret had the opening line of the play. Everything was set up onstage as it would be the following Saturday night, and after some initial problems with the technical crew, she got her cue and began. "'When shall we three meet again? In thunder, lightning, or in rain?'"

Bret was too absorbed in her role to notice whether Daniel was in the theater or not. As always when she acted, she was lost to thoughts of anything else. She simply became one of the witches who tempts Macbeth with the possibility of kingship.

Wrung out after her two brief scenes in Act I, she walked blindly offstage, fingering the bodice of her gown, which was a little tight. She gave a cry of surprise when she collided with a tall, jean-clad man whose arms went around her, trapping her hands against the soft material of a blue and green plaid flannel shirt.

"Double, double, you're in trouble, witch," he whispered crushing her so hard against him that her breasts were flattened by his pectoral muscles.

"Daniel!"

"You're an actress."

"I know." Her voice was muffled by the warm line of his throat. Held close to him, she felt the same sensual vertigo she'd experienced that morning in the garage. "I told you that the night we met."

"That is what you meant this morning by prophecies of doom? This is what you meant when you told me to come and watch you 'perform'?"

"Well, of course, Daniel. What else?" she said innocently.

"And this is where you come when you go to work?

All the evenings I've called you and gotten no answer, this is where you've been?"

"Rehearsing a play is time-consuming, Daniel. Particularly so close to opening night."

"You're not a witch or a medium or a psychic or a Gypsy fortune-teller?"

She shook her head. "Uh-uh. Graham does astrology part-time, and he sometimes works with a psychic. When she got sick last weekend he asked me to fill in for her. It's the first time I've ever done such a thing, and, considering the grief you gave me over it, it'll be the last." She leaned back in his arms and grinned up at him.

"You're laughing at me."

"You deserve it."

His dark eyebrows arched wickedly as one of his hands moved threateningly down to the curve of her bottom. "I'll get you for this. Nobody makes a fool out of me."

"I'm trembling."

"You should be. Why didn't you tell me before?"

"I tried to, several times, but you absolutely refused to listen. Anyway, I didn't want to spoil your fun. You seemed to take such pleasure in trying to intimidate me with your TV program. 'I'm going to lead you to a very public stake... and then I'm going to burn you!'" she quoted, mimicking his intonation perfectly.

"You're in big trouble, witch," he repeated with a grin. "For a solid week you've played havoc with my peace of mind with this little act of yours. I'm going to have my revenge."

His roughly sensual voice sent shivers through her, and she had to bite her tongue to stop herself from inviting him to go right ahead and avenge himself. However, she could tell from the spark in his eyes that he had read the invitation in her expression.

He leaned his head down but didn't kiss her. "What's

this gook all over your face?"

"Stage makeup, obviously. Don't mess it up; I've got another big scene later."

His eyes wandered to her bodice. "I like your costume," he said warmly. "Are you allowed to wear it home?"

"Of course not. It goes back to the costumers to be cleaned and pressed for opening night."

"It's very provocative. I'd like to have the pleasure of slowly unlacing it for you."

His heated words aroused her to an alarming degree. Once again things seemed to be rapidly escalating out of control. The chemistry between them was as potent as an incendiary bomb.

"Did you like my acting, Daniel?" she asked in a desperate attempt to change the subject.

"You're good," he said seriously. "You'd certainly tempt *me*."

"Stop it," she insisted, pushing his hands away from her bodice laces. "Do you have any idea what a costume like this costs?"

"No." His hands went instead to span her waist, and he smiled at her with eyes that were both teasing and lecherous. "What have you got on under it? I can't feel anything."

"A chastity belt," she retorted, pulling away from him. At this rate they'd be in bed before the evening was over. When he held her close, all her doubts and fears went flying out the window.

"You're a very beautiful and desirable witch, Bret Kingsley. And a terrific actress, too." He smiled. "I'm proud of you."

She flushed with his praise. The sexual electricity abated slightly as they met each other's eyes with a different kind of warmth. Yet again he had surprised her, reacting with good humor to the deception she'd foisted upon him all week. I like him, she thought in a sudden blaze of insight. I like him a lot.

"Thanks," she said aloud. Impulsively she squeezed his hand, then reached for a smock from a hook in the greenroom, donning it carefully to protect her costume. "Let's go out front and watch the play. I have to listen to what my director thinks of my performance. Unfortunately he's not liable to be so complimentary."

"He'd better be," Daniel growled. "Okay. I'm pretty fond of this play, as a matter of fact. Lead on, Macduff."

"Oh, Lord. Don't let the other actors hear you quoting from the play. It's bad luck. We're not even permitted to mention the production by name."

"Why not?"

"This play is haunted, of course. Terrible things happen to actors who play in it unless we're very careful."

Daniel gave her one of *those* looks. She recognized it from the night of the party. "You may not be a psychic, but you're clearly a kook," he said with a long-suffering sigh. "I must be out of my head, falling for you. I should have turned and run the other way the moment I saw you."

"On the contrary." She grinned at him. "Maybe I'm exactly what a stick-in-the-mud rationalist like you needs. Everybody should have some mystery, some magic, some witchcraft, in their lives."

His eyes caressed her with something more than passion. There was affection there, she was certain. He opened his mouth as if to speak, then shook his head faintly and smiled instead. "Come on. Let's watch the haunted play, my love."

The possessive way he'd said "my love" warmed her for the rest of the evening.

"You really shouldn't do anything adventuresome tonight, luv," Graham said to her as she was hanging up her costume after the rehearsal. Daniel was waiting for her outside. "Baleful planetary influences, you know. According to the charts, a Pisces like you should lock all the doors and windows and crawl safely into bed...alone. It's definitely not the time to take any risks."

"Oh, great. That makes me feel terrific, Graham."

"And whatever you do, don't travel. Not that you need an astrologer to tell you that. Just look out the window."

It was still snowing. In fact, during the hours they'd been in the theater, a fierce nor'easter had struck the city, dumping several inches of new snow and threatening a good deal more. "I have to travel to get home," she pointed out. "So do you, for heaven's sake."

"Go home, by all means. Just don't go anywhere else."

She caught her lower lip in her teeth in a brief nervous gesture. "You don't like Daniel, do you?"

"I don't care for the way he looks at you, no."

"You were the one who abandoned me to him last weekend at that party. You blithely told him I was a witch and took off!"

"I was an idiot. He'll walk all over you, Bret."

"He's a Scorpio. You said we were compatible."

"Scorpios are ruled by the planet Pluto, who was the god of the underworld, if you remember. They're hard, dark, and fierce. And they're hell on women. Remember what happened to Persephone when Pluto decided he wanted her? He thundered up out of the ground in his chariot and dragged her screaming down to Hades."

"He released her when her mother went crazy with grief and brought winter to the world."

"Only because the other gods insisted. And, even so, he demanded that she spend half of every year with him. She had eaten his food; that was what condemned her." He looked dramatically out the window at the raging snow. "She's with him now, languishing in heavy darkness, held in thrall by that overpowering sensuality all Pluto people possess."

"For heaven's sake, Graham!"

"Why don't you find yourself a nice Cancer? That's the other sign you're compatible with, and they're much safer, believe me."

"I like Daniel," she said stubbornly.

"You're going to sleep with him, aren't you?"

The little throbs of excitement that had shivered in her all evening erupted again. Her heart was beating twice as fast as usual, and her skin felt so sensitive that she was aware of every inch of her clothes. She fussed with her costume and didn't answer.

She heard the crack of Graham's knuckles and heard him moving close behind her. "Remember me," he said quietly, touching her shoulder. "I'm the one who'll be here to pick up the pieces when it's over."

She turned spontaneously and hugged him. "It'll be okay, Graham," she said. "Don't worry about me."

Graham kissed her forehead, then pushed her away. "Go on. He's waiting."

A half hour later she and Daniel were standing on her front porch, shaking themselves like bedraggled animals and stamping the snow off their boots.

"You'd better invite me in this time, lady, or I'm liable to turn into the Abominable Snowman."

She laughed as she struggled with her keys. "Not even I could be so cruel as to send you home on a night like this without a nightcap or a cup of hot coffee."

When she finally managed the lock, Daniel pushed the door open, and they stepped together into the house. "Ah-ha," she thought she heard him say as he moved into the warmth of her front hall. He pushed back his hood and tore off his gloves, and before she could blink his snowy jacket was unzipped.

"The vampire is in!" he crowed, backing her against the nearest wall. He tipped up her chin with his fingers and thumb and stared at her parted lips for an instant. "You're doomed," he added huskily before covering her mouth with his.

Chapter 5

BRET MELTED INTO the kiss as surely as the dusting of snow from their jackets melted and dripped into tiny puddles on the floor. Daniel's lips were hotly possessive, his body strong and all-encompassing. *I want you so,* she said silently as she slid her hands up his arms to tangle her fingers in the damp, dark waves of his hair. He was delicious—a warm, vital force, a dynamic whirlwind of masculinity.

"Mmm," he murmured against her mouth. His tongue completed a lazy washing of her lips that made her entire body glow. "I've been dreaming about this all evening. All day. I've been walking around in a daze of desire since this morning, my love." He stripped himself and then her of their coats and scarves in a few economical moves. One hand skated down her throat, opening the top three buttons of the green silk blouse she wore over her jeans, and he lightly massaged the hollow between her breasts. "I've been aching to do this," he whispered. His thumb splayed out and rasped over a nipple. She shivered and curled closer to him. "And this," he added, coaxing the nipple to hardness with rough yet tender fingers. "There are so many things I want to do with you tonight."

"Me, too," she admitted, leaning her head against his throat. "But"—she hesitated as her earlier reservations came rushing back—"I told you, Daniel. I just can't take this sort of thing lightly."

"No one's asking you to take it lightly." He moved her head slightly so he could nibble on her earlobe and run his tongue along the hairline where her thick tresses sprang. "My feelings for you could hardly be characterized as light."

"Rumor has it that you go through a lot of women," she whispered. A moment later she wished it unsaid. It sounded like a demand that he offer her something more than he usually offered his bedmates.

"Don't listen to rumors." His hands moved down her back and curved over the soft flesh of her bottom, cupping her tightly against his thighs. "Trust me. I'm really quite an honest man, you know."

"I remember. One of your good points." She leaned back and smiled saucily at him. He immediately unhooked one of her hands from around his neck and held the palm up for examination.

"What of *your* heartline, witch? Are our palms as compatible as our horoscopes?" He brought her hand to his lips and ran his tongue over her palm. The sensual muscles inside her convulsed, and she felt as if her legs were going to give way. A soft sound of pleasure rose in her throat as his clever tongue slid in between each of her fingers, circled the base of her thumb, then devilishly probed the sensitive hollow in the center of her palm.

"Daniel," she whispered.

He dropped her hand and kissed her mouth again with a passion that she matched blindly, fiercely, and without thought—until Chester meowed and shoved his body between their legs.

"What the hell?"

"It's okay. It's only Chester. I think he's jealous." She stooped down to ruffle the tawny creature behind the ears. "Hi, baby. I want you to meet Daniel."

Chester rubbed his head against his mistress's fingers and pointedly ignored Daniel, who stared down at him, saying, "That's the biggest cat I've ever seen. Is he domesticated?"

"Just barely," she laughed.

Daniel gamely attempted to pet Chester, but the huge yellow tomcat lurched out of his way, swatting the telephone table with his tail. The phone fell to the floor with a crash, dial tone buzzing. Bret picked it up while Chester slunk away into the kitchen. "He's very clumsy. Fortunately this phone is one of the telephone company's sturdier models."

"I don't think he likes me," Daniel said as Chester gave him a haughty amber-eyed stare from the kitchen doorway.

"He's suspicious of men. He doesn't see very many."

One of Daniel's hands lightly clamped her wrist. "I find that a little hard to believe, Bret."

"Well, it's true." She tried to withdraw her arm, but it was held fast by his strong fingers. She leaned her head back and opened her eyes wide. "What's the matter—getting possessive already, Haggarty?"

"Did you miss that in my palm, witch? I've been possessive of you from the moment we met."

His gruffly assertive tone thrilled her at the same time

that it made her a trifle wary. She had no experience dealing with a willful, passionate man like Daniel. Arthur had been so even-tempered and serene.

He'll try to dominate you, Graham had warned that first night. Scorpio men were famous for that. And Bret knew that, good-natured though she was, she lacked the submissive spirit of some Pisces women. If Daniel tried to dominate her, they would end up fighting.

She and Arthur had never fought. In retrospect, it seemed rather odd. How could you live so long with someone and never disagree?

"I hope it's not these supposedly nonexistent other men you're brooding about," Daniel prompted, watching her face.

"Actually I'm brooding about Arthur. I assure you, there are no other men."

"Do you often brood about Arthur?"

She bristled a little. "Not often, no. You are possessive, aren't you?"

There was a taut silence before the tension in him suddenly dissolved. He ran a hand through his black hair, unconsciously mussing it. "I'm sorry." His charcoal eyes glinted with self-deprecation. "I suppose I'm what you might call a very territorial male."

"Hmm. You and Chester probably have a lot in common." At the sound of his name, Chester meowed plaintively. "He's hungry," Bret explained, moving down the hall to the kitchen, where Chester was expectantly circling his supper dish. Daniel followed, bumping his head on the low archway to the kitchen and cursing. Chester glared at him with what strongly resembled satisfaction.

"Be careful," she warned too late. "It's an old house."

Daniel looked around the modern kitchen. "Looks pretty contemporary in here."

"We renovated the kitchen and the bathrooms. Actually we had to renovate the entire house before we could live comfortably here—new floors, new windows, insulation, a new heating system, new plumbing and wiring." She opened a cupboard and took down a can of cat food. Chester was rubbing up against her. "It was quite a project."

"*We* refers to you and Arthur, I presume? You lived here with him?"

"Yes."

There was a short silence. Daniel leaned back against one of the countertops and folded his arms across his chest, carefully considering her as she dumped the cat food into Chester's dish and placed it on the floor. Chester pounced.

"What happened to Arthur anyway? How did he die?"

"He was killed in a car accident. I was in the car, too," Bret informed him in a flat voice. "He swerved to avoid a child who had run into the road, and we crashed into a tree."

Daniel crossed to her, cursing softly as he took her in his arms. He cradled her face in gentle hands. "I'm so sorry."

"Arthur was thrown from the car and died instantly when his head struck a rock. I was trapped—they had to use the Jaws of Life to get me out." She shuddered, remembering. "Afterward, when they told me about Arthur, I didn't want to go on living. But I wasn't hurt badly enough to die."

"Thank God for that."

He held her close for several minutes while she regained her composure. She could feel his compassion washing over her. His hands massaged her shoulders and fiddled with her hair.

"I'm okay now," she said, pulling away from him. She carefully covered the cat-food can with aluminum foil and put it away, suddenly feeling uncomfortable under his steady gaze. "Do you want a drink?" she asked, pulling open the cupboard over the oven to reveal her small cache of alcoholic beverages. "I think I have some cognac."

"No, I don't want a drink. Am I making you nervous?" he added when she turned and inadvertently bumped her head against the cabinet door.

"Nervous?" She smiled, determined not to appear edgy, but she found herself taking an automatic step backward as he advanced toward her. She felt the edge of the sink against the small of her back as his hands settled on the counter on either side of her, trapping her. He was too close—his hot breath on her face, the coiled power of his hard-muscled body only centimeters away. She felt caged, cornered.

"How long has it been, Bret?" His voice was low, sensual.

She turned her head away from his tantalizing eyes and mouth and stared out the small kitchen window at the darkly falling snow. "What do you mean?" she asked. But she knew.

"There's really been no one since Arthur died? You haven't had a man in three years?"

"I suppose that must seem pretty weird to someone like you."

His fingers trailed over her cheek, caressed the curve of her mouth. "Not necessarily weird. You loved your husband. I can understand that. But it does seem an enormous waste." He lowered his head until his lips whispered over hers, "A beautiful, vibrant woman like you shouldn't lock herself away from the males of the world. It only makes us more determined to seek you out and make you feel alive again."

He kissed her deeply then, but she fought him, not knowing why. He had upset her somehow, scared her. He could bring her body to a riot of wild sensations, but she sensed he would demand much more from her than he would be willing to give in return. All Graham's warnings came back to haunt her. She was Persephone, tempted to the feast by the dark lord of the underworld . . . but if she gave in, and ate, she would be forever subject to his will.

As she continued to resist, his kiss became gentler, more seductive. When her mouth refused to open to him, the tip of his tongue flicked her, coaxed her, entreated rather than demanded. "Nothing's going to happen unless you want it to," he murmured against her lips. "But I can't seem to stop trying to make you want it. It's my nature, I'm afraid."

"Sex is important to you." She felt her resolve weakening as fine wires of sensation curled through her.

He moved his hips against her. "Yes."

"Dear God," she whispered as the floodgates inside her suddenly gave way. Her fingers moved lightly over his shoulders, feeling the strong contours of hard muscle and sinew beneath the flannel of his shirt. She swallowed hard. "I need more than that, dammit!" she insisted. "I wouldn't be valuing myself as a person if I pretended I didn't."

"Let's sit down, okay?" With one arm cradling her to his side, he steered her into the living room and dropped them both down on the plump-cushioned ivory-colored couch. He gathered her close, practically into his lap, but his beguiling caresses ceased. She felt his chin rest on the top of her head as he said, "I need more than that, too. I told you that this morning in the car."

"You also told me you couldn't make any promises. Which makes sense, of course," she hastened to add. "We hardly know each other."

"We know each other. We looked into each other's eyes on the night we met and intuitively learned all the important stuff right then and there."

"I don't believe it! D. D. Haggarty, professional rationalist, proclaiming the virtues of intuitive communication?"

She could feel him smile. "Not exactly. It's all due to the sense of smell, you know. Perfectly rational and scientific. Intuition has nothing to do with it."

"Smell?" she repeated, sniffing dubiously. He did have a pleasant natural scent about him, she had to admit. A faint glimmering of woodsy maleness.

"Yes. Haven't you heard that explanation of instant attraction? It's no longer termed love at first sight, but a bonding of the olfactory senses. My nose and yours are soul mates."

Bret giggled. He lifted her chin and rubbed his nose back and forth against hers. "You see? They're crazy about each other."

The conjunction of noses brought their mouths within a whisper of one another. Bret's chest tightened as he said against her moistened lips, "It sounds crazy, even to me, but I honestly feel that there's a lot more at stake with you than there's been with any other woman in my life."

"At stake? As in burning at the?"

He lowered his lips to her throat, letting her feel his teeth. The tiny threat made her breathless. "Cute, Bret. Why do I have the feeling you're not taking me seriously?"

I'm afraid I'm taking you all too seriously. You're too passionately emotional, too dynamic, and much too sexy for me not to take you seriously, D. D. Haggarty. You're tearing my quiet existence to shreds!

"You promised you wouldn't press me, Daniel."

He smiled wistfully. "Did I say that? I'm a fool." He pulled her closer, nestling her head against his shoulder. "Do you want me to go?"

She felt the warm, solid length of him beside her, his hands gently caressing her, his comfortable shoulder, his strong thighs just beside hers on the sofa—all the things that testified to his incredible sex appeal. If he stayed, they would make love. In all honesty, wasn't that what she wanted?

He shifted, pressing her back against the arm of the sofa, fitting one long leg between hers so she could feel his hard muscles against her inner thighs. At the same time one of his hands settled lightly over one of her breasts, reminding her of how wonderful it could be between them.

"No fair," she whispered.

"This is entirely your decision," he returned, his lips moving deliciously on her throat. "Far be it from me to try to influence you."

She groaned and circled his neck with her arms. There was no real doubt about it, of course. She was about to agree to anything he wanted when Chester pounced, landing squarely on Daniel's back and digging in his claws.

"Dammit, not again!" Daniel rolled defensively off the couch, and Chester neatly took his place on Bret's chest, flopping down against the warmth of her body and beginning to purr loudly. On his knees on the Oriental rug beside the couch, Daniel glared at the two of them— Bret, who was laughing, and Chester, who was giving Bret an indignant look as if to demand why her comfy breasts were shaking up and down.

"I'll kill the beast," he vowed, grabbing the orange tomcat and putting him down firmly, but not roughly, on the floor. Chester yowled in protest. "He's territorial all right. Good God, he looks as if he's planning to fight me for you." He reached awkwardly over his shoulder to rub the spot where Chester had landed. "You never warned me he was trained to attack. He's fierce as a lion."

Bret's laughter escalated. "Daniel in the lion's den!"

"Very funny."

She controlled herself sufficiently to ask if Chester's claws had done any real damage. "Let me see," she said, pulling Daniel down beside her again and working the buttons on the front of his plaid shirt. She bit her lip as she watched the tangles of curly black chest hair emerge. She couldn't seem to help running her fingers over his chest, pressing them deep into the springy curls. "Take it off," she said, dry-mouthed.

"Are you kidding? With him running around loose? That thick shirt's the only thing that saved me just now." But his dark eyes were flaring with barely contained passion.

"Let me see your back."

He turned, slipping the shirt off his shoulders. Beneath his smooth skin, muscle could be faintly seen to ripple, but there were no deep scratches, only a few red marks. "I think you'll live, Haggarty," Bret said, her voice husky from the longing she had to run her hands over the naked flesh before her.

He turned back and met her eyes. Sparks sizzled between them, and the wires tightened within Bret's body. It was going to happen. She couldn't stop it.

Chester prowled around the sofa, eyeing Bret's cozy body and Daniel's bare back. Daniel shot the cat a cautious look. "He's planning his move. He's going to pounce when I least expect it—and I can just imagine the moment he'll choose. I'm beginning to think you've lured me in here so Chester could finish me off, witch." He sidled up against her and ran the tip of one finger from her collarbone down along the open buttons of her blouse, between her breasts and across her stomach to the snap that closed her jeans. "Put him out, Bret."

"There's a blizzard outside."

"Then come with me to my place. I'd prefer it that way. If I'm going to be the first man to make love to you since Arthur's death, I want it to be special for you." He glanced around the room of her old Victorian house. "I don't want to do it in the house where you lived with him. Come home with me tonight, Bret."

She could feel her heartbeat kick and scamper in her throat. "Daniel, the driving's terrible tonight."

"I live in Winchester—it's not far away. My car handles well in the snow." When she hesitated he added, "Humor me. I feel very strongly about this."

"But what if the snow keeps up and I get stranded? I have rehearsals tomorrow."

"Dear God, tomorrow's Sunday. Don't they ever give you people a break?"

"Not just before a new production opens."

"I'll get you back, I promise. Besides—" He was drawing breath to continue, but he ended up turning his face away and sneezing explosively. "Dammit," he swore, unsuccessfully searching his pockets for a handkerchief as he sneezed again.

She caressed his hair. "It's cold and wet out there, Daniel. Let's stay here and build a fire. Your hair is damp, and your cold'll get worse if we go out again."

"I don't have a cold." Bending over, he sneezed again, six times in rapid succession. "There's only one thing in the world that could cause this." He turned his glare accusingly on the huge mound of tawny fluff who was hostilely contemplating him from the other side of the coffee table.

"Oh, no," Bret moaned. "Chester."

"Chester," Daniel repeated with a scowl before sneezing again.

Bret disentangled herself and got up from the sofa to coax the unsuspecting Chester into her arms. She rubbed his head vigorously as she carried him toward the front hall. "I'll put him out."

But when she opened the door, Chester took one look at the swirling snow and heaved himself out of her arms. *Crash.* He knocked over the umbrella stand near the front door as he tore off in a blur of orange. But he didn't anticipate Daniel, who brought him down on the living room carpet with an impressive football tackle.

"And if you claw me again, you moth-eaten excuse for a cat, I'll drown you!" Daniel assured him as he hefted the creature and carried him gingerly back to the front door. "He's as slippery as you are," he added, having quite a time holding on to the spitting animal. "Get those claws away from me—ow!"

"What's the matter?" Bret demanded a moment later when Daniel slammed the door with Chester still on the inside.

He sneezed and looked a little sheepish. "I can't do it. I can't just heave him out into the snow."

"You can't?"

"It's miserable out there, isn't it, you monster," he said, rubbing a relieved-looking Chester behind the ears. "Don't fret; it's your house, after all, buddy."

As she stared dumbfoundedly at the handsome, sneezing devil cuddling the cat he was allergic to, Bret once again knew that she liked Daniel Haggarty very much indeed. Their eyes met, and warmth drifted through her. It was a different kind of warmth from the sensual heat he inspired, although that was there, too. It was a quiet, intimate communion between two sympathetic hearts and minds—a golden, timeless moment she wished would never end. And she knew that Daniel was right: On some very profound level they did know all the important things about each other.

Daniel set the cat down as his vigorous sneezing started up again. Once again he patted his pocket. "Wouldn't you know it? I forgot to bring my medication. Do you suppose there's a drugstore open around here?"

"You needn't suffer." She reached for his hand. "I'll come with you to your place. Give me a couple of minutes to get ready."

The banked fires in Daniel's eyes leaped to flame again. "What about Chester?"

"He's got a cat box and lots of food. He'll be all right here for the night."

Daniel smiled wickedly. "So the damn allergy is good for something at last."

Chester was lying on the rug in front of the fire when Bret came downstairs with her overnight bag, but there was no sign of Daniel until she heard a muffled sneeze from the small study that opened off the living room. Arthur's study. All his things—books, papers, personal effects—were still in there. She'd never had the heart to sort through them and decide what to keep and what to throw away.

"What are you doing?" she demanded, finding Daniel examining a photo of herself and Arthur on vacation in Montreal.

"Trying to escape from your cat." His voice was faintly sarcastic as he added, "I'm sorry—is the shrine off limits?"

"It's not a shrine."

"Arthur Kingsley, M.S.W.," he read from one of the degrees mounted on the beige-papered wall. "What was he, a social worker?"

"Yes. He worked with inner-city kids."

"A noble profession," Daniel said in a neutral tone. He picked up a wedding photograph in a silver, heart-shaped frame and examined it. "He was a good-looking guy," he said, staring at Arthur's blond, lanky form. "Very attractive."

Bret took the wedding picture away from him and placed it back on Arthur's desk. She treasured that photograph. She and Arthur had had the heart-shaped frame specially made. She felt almost protective of it, and she didn't want Daniel to touch it.

She watched uneasily as he continued his exploration of the room, running his fingers over the volumes in the bookcase. His mood had changed again. Dear heavens, what a volatile man he was!

He picked up a journal. "The Proceedings of the

American Society of Spiritualists?" He shot her a dark look. "What's this doing here, Bret?"

"My mother gave me a subscription for Christmas last year."

"Ah, yes. Your fascinating mother." His tone had subtly hardened. He picked up a deck of tarot cards and shuffled them idly. "It's clear where your talents as an actress come from. That's all you share with her, I hope?"

"What are you getting at, Daniel? I thought we were leaving."

He waved his hand at the wedding picture and Arthur's effects. "We are. There's one thing I want to settle first, though, Bret. You know now that I'm possessive. This mausoleum annoys me."

Bret felt herself flush with irritation. "Do you have a mania for spoiling things, Haggarty?"

"I'm sorry, but I think it's important. I don't want to make love to a married woman."

"Married!"

"I know the sort of people who subscribe to these journals; I've researched the subject, remember. A faithful widow for over three years . . . It reminds me of many cases I've investigated. The surviving spouse who simply can't accept the fact of her partner's death." His face had turned rigid with his "Scorpio brooder" expression. "How often do you go to seances, Bret? How often do you have cozy little conversations through a medium with your dear deceased Arthur?"

Bret's breath left her in a gasp. Her eyes closed automatically. "I don't go to seances. You can be very cruel sometimes, Daniel."

When he spoke again it was from right beside her. "Maybe. But it's cruel of you to ask me to compete for your attention with a ghost."

"I'm not asking any such thing! I'm not a spiritualist, for godsake!"

"I once heard you talking aloud to Arthur," he persisted. His hands had fallen heavily upon her shoulders, holding her still for his questioning. She had a sudden image of herself sitting before a video camera, being interrogated by this sometimes ruthless man.

"Talking to Arthur?" she repeated blankly.

"On the stairs, after the party, on the night we met. You were saying you missed him."

She remembered his sardonic remark about communicating with the spirit world.

"In my experience, people who talk to the dead are either crazy or duped."

"How about lonely?" she burst out, tearing herself away from him. "Or have you never known what *that* feels like?"

He stared at her in ominous silence for several seconds before saying, "Swear to me you're not involved in spirit circles, Bret. It's the one thing I don't think I could take."

"Why not? What the hell have you got against spiritualism, anyway? You're a fanatic on the subject!"

"With good reason," he said starkly.

"*What* good reason? It better be a damn good reason, because I resent being hounded by you, Daniel! Dear God, a few minutes ago you wanted to make love to me!"

His eyes seemed to darken as he stared into hers, the charcoal-gray irises retreating as the pupils dilated. "I still want to make love to you. There's nothing I want more. But I won't share you with anybody, least of all a ghost!"

She drew a deep breath. She didn't understand this side of him. It had disturbed her from the start, and she knew with every ounce of intuition she possessed that there was going to be trouble between them because of her mother, her crazy upbringing, and even her personal beliefs in the extraordinary powers of the human mind. She wondered what Daniel would think if she told him about her childhood, growing up in a haunted house.

How could she ever explain to him about those years? He would think she was lying.

She sighed. "I'm not a spiritualist, Daniel. I still occasionally miss my husband, but he's dead and I'm alive. I've accepted that. I'm sorry if I seem to you to be carrying around an excess of emotional baggage from my marriage. I'm trying to shed it. It may still take a while; I may still have to ask you to be patient. If that's too much to ask"—she paused, not wanting to say it, but feeling it necessary to make the point—"there are other women around, Daniel."

His hands were on her once more, and she could feel his tension. "I don't want any other woman. I want you."

"You have me," she whispered. "My suitcase is packed, and I'm going home with you tonight."

His fingers tightened slightly, and she felt dizzy with awareness of his sheer physical power. She wondered vaguely why she felt no fear of him. Emotionally he frightened her, but not physically. He was much taller and stronger than she, but in that realm, at least, she trusted him. It must have been so from the moment they met, or she never would have accepted a ride from a dark stranger on an even darker night.

"Don't ask for patience from me, Bret," he said. "When I get you into my house, into my bed, I won't be capable of restraint. If you come with me tonight, I'll possess you, and nothing in heaven or earth will stop me."

She raised her hands to his face and touched the feathering of hair above his ears. "Patience with my emotions, not with my person," she whispered huskily. "I give the latter to you freely."

He sighed and pulled her almost savagely close. She could feel his accelerated heartbeat against her breasts. One of his hands slid into the hair at her nape and forced her head back. He kissed her hard, his tongue invading her with a furious passion, which she met with the surge of her own body. She was alive, all right, very much alive. She could feel Daniel's warmth flowing into her body, making every cell cry out with the joy of its animation.

Breathing unsteadily, Daniel disengaged himself enough to see her passion-flushed face. "You turn my bones to water, you know that?"

"They'll be turning to ice if we get stuck out on the highway in this blizzard," she said lightly.

"Let's go," he agreed, taking her arm and leading her out of the study. She caught one last glimpse of her wedding picture as she shut the study door behind them. She spoke again to Arthur, silently this time. "Wish me luck," she told him, which seemed kinder than "Good-bye."

Chapter

6

THE DRIVING WAS AWFUL. Bret sat huddled in the seat next to Daniel, staring through the ice-coated windshield and trying by sheer force of will to keep the car from skidding off the road. Massachusetts Avenue in Cambridge was barely plowed, and the conditions worsened as they drove through Arlington. Center toward Winchester, the wealthy suburb where Daniel had his home.

Once, when the car skidded ninety degrees to the left before straightening out, Daniel reached to cover her hand with his. "Scared?"

"A little."

"I'm sorry. It's snowing much harder than it was an hour ago. Nothing's going to happen—I promise. We're going to get there, safe and sound. Do you trust me?"

His tone inspired confidence. He seemed so powerful, so capable. "Yes."

His mouth turned up in a lecherous grin. "Big mistake, lady. You're going to be snowed in with me—trapped and completely at my mercy."

She grinned back, waves of excitement churning within her despite her nervousness about the storm. "Try anything, and I'll put a spell on you, Haggarty."

"Put a spell on me, darling, and I'll bite your neck."

Nearly one hour after leaving Cambridge they finally pulled into the long drive that led to Daniel's house. There their luck ran out. A small tree was down, blocking their way. "Everybody out," said Daniel cheerfully. "We hike the rest of the way."

The snowfall was even heavier in Winchester than it had been in Cambridge, but the worst hazard was the ice-sharp wind, which drifted the snow unpredictably. Needles of snow cut into their faces, and before they had gone more than a hundred yards, Bret's hands and feet were numb.

"How much farther?" she gasped, clinging to Daniel's arm with fingers that seemed to lack any connection to her body.

"What?" he yelled back.

"Where's the blasted house?"

"We're almost there," he promised over and over while pulling her along, forcing her to keep walking what felt like miles.

Courage, she told herself bracingly as she wondered if her toes would survive the trek. "There is a house, isn't there?" she asked, trying to hide her anxiety. "I really don't care to traipse through a blizzard all night." Or collapse here and freeze, she added silently.

She saw him bend over her and felt his warm mouth against her own. "Don't fade on me now," he whispered. "You're strong; you swim every morning."

"I'm not fading," she insisted even as she burrowed closer against him for warmth.

He pushed her away gently, keeping one arm around

her waist. "It's warm inside, love. Hurry up."

"Graham warned me not to travel tonight," she muttered. "I should have listened to him." She couldn't see a thing through the whirling blizzard, but she kept walking—or dragging, rather—sweating under her coat from the effort and shivering simultaneously as the wind chilled her. She was seriously considering taking a nice rest in the comfortable snow, but just then they rounded a curve and she saw the house before them—a huge silhouette with one light gleaming like a beacon.

"Thank God," said Daniel, and with a renewed burst of energy he hoisted her up into his arms and carried her the rest of the way.

She put her face against his neck and murmured, "You're crazy. I'm perfectly capable of walking."

"Don't argue. Think of it as an abduction: He lifts her high in his arms and strides forcefully down the hall to the master bedroom..."

"I always wonder why the guy doesn't get a hernia. Daniel, please! I may look thin, but that's on a five-foot eight-inch frame. Do you know how much I weigh?"

"I know I'll never send you chocolates again. There. Whew." He dumped her unceremoniously to her feet on the front porch and unlocked the door. "Come on in. Don't stop to look around; just head for the stairs."

"Yes sir," she said, rubbing her hands vigorously to warm them. But she couldn't help a few expressions of delight as he led her through a large, airy front hall lit by a crystal chandelier to the curved staircase, which rose elegantly to the second floor. "Heavens, the place is a mansion," she said, noting the quality of the art on the wall. "Are you rich, Haggarty?" She abruptly remembered the hundred-dollar bill he'd donated to the National Foundation for the Blind. "TV must pay an awful lot better than repertory."

"You don't care much about money, do you, Bret?" She could honestly say she didn't. "I wouldn't turn my nose up at it, but, no, it's not something I waste time thinking about."

"My father cared about little else," he explained as they mounted the stairs after shedding their coats and boots at the bottom. "He literally worked himself into the ground making it, lots of it. He died many years ago. My mother, too. I was their only child. All the fruits of his labors came to me, including this house."

"You sound bitter."

"The house is beautiful, as are many of the things in it. But I'd rather have had my parents."

She squeezed his hand. He moved her heart in ways she wouldn't allow herself to put a name to. How could she care so much, so soon?

He led her down a cherrywood-paneled hallway to the bedroom at the far end. It was cozily masculine, papered in autumn tones, a large, old-fashioned room with an antique bureau, a rolltop desk, and a couple of easy chairs in front of a mammoth fireplace. But it was the huge four-poster bed that really caught Bret's attention. It was covered with a flame-colored spread, which seemed so appropriate to Daniel's nature that she laughed out loud.

"The sizzling setting for your seduction," he whispered just behind her, his breath hot against her ear. His hands rested lightly on her shoulders, then moved down slowly, deliberately, to cup her breasts. "Still cold?"

"Uh, yes, a little."

"We should have stayed at your place, cat or no cat. I'm sorry, love. I had no idea the driving would be so bad."

His fingers were doing wonderful things to her. "It's okay," she managed. "We made it."

He chuckled. "Not yet we haven't." His fingers slipped lower to the waistband of her jeans. "These'll have to come off. They're wet."

Her pants were soaked from her thighs down. Daniel's hands hovered at her waist, awaiting her signal. "Oh, all right," she agreed. She could feel his tension as he somewhat awkwardly unfastened them. He hesitated a moment before he pushed them over her hips and off, leaving the lower half of her body naked except for a pair of bikini panties. The touch of his hands electrified her. Her skin felt sensitized, alive.

"Come on," he said, taking her hand. He walked her across the room to a door on the left and into the bathroom, which was as large as a bedroom in any normal house and as thoroughly modern as the house itself was antique. It was equipped with a sunken bathtub that was unquestionably the biggest Bret had ever seen.

"You could keep a whale in there," she noted in awe.

Daniel skirted the tub and led her to a door on the other side of the double marble sinks. "A sauna," he explained, fiddling with a dial on the door. "This should take the chill off."

"A *sauna?* Good grief, Haggarty, you live like a king."

"Take off the rest of your clothes."

She slowly unbuttoned her blouse, looked expectantly at him, trying to convey the idea that a tactful man might consider leaving her alone, at least briefly. He didn't take the hint. Instead, he jerked his own shirt out of his waistband and started to unfasten it.

"Daniel, what are you doing?" She gulped, staring at the rapidly emerging sight of his strong chest muscles dusted with glossy black hair. The plaid shirt came off, then the gold watch around his wrist. He unbuckled the leather belt at his waist.

"What does it look like I'm doing?" His tone had roughened.

"I thought we'd just sort of take things slowly and—"

He whipped off the belt and leaned closer to kiss her firmly on the mouth. "Nothing will happen too fast. I promise you. Anyway, this is therapeutic; we're both badly chilled. Are you going to take the rest of those clothes off, or do I have to do it for you?"

She hesitated for a moment more. Coward, she told herself impatiently. You've come this far; this is no time to start having second thoughts.

"I'll do it." She slipped out of her blouse and added it to the pile. She was left in a matching bra and panties of sheer material, and she knew without even meeting his eyes that Daniel was watching her, his gaze licking over her, kindling sparks everywhere it touched.

She heard him suck in his breath and take a step closer. He was very near now; she could feel the heat he was radiating. Her heartbeat slammed into high gear.

Daniel touched one hand to her flat stomach, his thumb nudging her navel. "Great stomach muscles," he said huskily. The hand slid up to the undercurve of one breast. In instant response her nipples puckered out against the silken cups of her bra. "Ah," he breathed. "You're lovely, sweetheart. I can hardly believe you're here, finally, in my keeping."

As he drew her against his naked chest she thought what an odd, old-fashioned word that was: his *keeping*. It made her feel special, cared for, cherished. Their coming together in the parking garage this morning had been raw sexual passion, unalloyed with gentler emotions, but there was more between them now.

His hands moved around behind her back, seeking the clasp of her bra. In a whisper of sound the flimsy garment slipped down her arms and off. He cupped her breasts in the palms of his hands and rubbed them up and down against his chest.

The feel of his dark springy hair against her delicate skin sent spasms through her. She sighed and leaned into the caress. Daniel's thumbs skated deliciously over her nipples, urging them to even greater arousal. They ached and peaked against him.

He pushed her back a little, his eyes drinking her in. "Your breasts are beautiful. I knew they would be."

"Somehow I don't think this is very therapeutic," she murmured, gazing up at him through half-closed eyelids.

"Oh, I don't know. We're doing a nice job of staving off hypothermia." His hands eased down her backbone to the base of her spine and pulled her lower body into the cradle of his thighs. She had just a hint of his arousal before she wriggled away, exclaiming, "Your jeans are wet!"

He stepped back and began to tug them off. "Last one in is condemned to be the other's slave for the entire night."

Moments later Bret sprawled nude on a wooden bench inside the sauna, laughing through the door at Daniel's attempts to peel the stiff, water-logged jeans from his legs. "I've always wanted a sexy male slave."

But when he joined her, his body magnificently toned and very blatantly aroused, she felt a thrill of apprehension. The intense cold of the trek through the snow was rapidly fading into unreality as that drugged, dizzy feeling she'd experienced in the garage took hold of her again. If anybody was going to be enslaved, she thought dazedly, it was almost certain to be she.

As promised, Daniel didn't allow anything to happen too fast. With tantalizing slowness he lowered his body to the bench beside her, stretching his legs lazily. He didn't touch her. "This is great, isn't it? Are you warming up?"

"Um-hmm." If he tried to measure her sexual temperature, she thought wryly, the thermometer would explode.

He turned slightly toward her and shifted her until her back was nestled against his chest. Just the light touch of his hands on her arms, moving her, ordering her position, made her tremble with anticipation.

She leaned her head back against his shoulder. Her long hair brushed his chest, and he fondled it, running strands of it through his fingers. Catlike, she arched her back.

One of his hands dropped to her breasts, slowly molding one, then the other. Her skin was beginning to dampen from the heat, and his fingers slipped over it easily, exploring and teasing and probing. "You have the most beautiful breasts," he repeated. "They fit my hands so perfectly."

She couldn't speak.

He moved in closer behind her. "Bend forward a little," he instructed her.

She brought her legs up on the bench in front of her and bent from the waist, resting her head on her raised knees. This made her breasts fall fully into Daniel's hands, and he took merciless advantage of their position. After kneading, caressing, and pressing them together, he began to work on the erect nipples, rolling them between his fingers and gently tugging on them until she thought she would die. Every touch reverberated in the pit of her stomach, flooding her loins with unbearable heat. Before more than a couple of minutes had passed, she was squirming on the bench, longing for assuagement.

"I'm hot, Haggarty," she murmured. "I need to cool off."

"Mmm." He was kneeling behind her now, and his lips were nudging the nape of her neck. She could feel the slight coarseness of his five o'clock shadow against her tender skin. "That can be arranged."

She was conscious of tiny sparks of excitement mixing with the heat of the sauna to make her liquid all over. She could hear the sound of his accelerated breathing, could feel the beating of his heart beneath her shoulder blade.

His fingers slid over her belly to crinkle the down at the apex of her thighs. Then he touched in between her legs, lightly, delicately. "You're beautiful here, too," he told her. She felt him shudder, and he withdrew his hand. His naked body was taut and silky against her. She heard him curse softly. "I'm trying to go slowly, but . . ."

She twisted in his arms, turning to face him and kneeling up on the sauna bench to brush a lock of damp hair out of his eyes. "It's okay," she reassured him. "I'm ready for you, Daniel."

He folded her against him, whispering, "I want to make it good for you, sweetheart. I want your first time after three years to be special." He nuzzled her throat, his teeth teasing an earlobe. "Come on, let's get out of here before we faint."

Under the shower in the enormous bathtub they washed the sweat off each other . . . ever so carefully. Bret longed to run her hands all over his firm, aroused body, but she knew he was too near the edge to be teased. His barely restrained passion excited her further. He was as taut as an arched bow and as devastating in his potential power. It awed and amazed her that all this pure masculine energy should be focused on her.

When they stepped out of the shower and she tried to dry him with one of the huge bathsheets, he pushed her away and did it himself, motioning her to do the same and staring at her with such naked lust in his eyes that she felt another tiny frisson of apprehension. He was so intense!

When she was dry he caught her wrist and fairly dragged her out of the bathroom toward the huge bed that loomed on the other side of the bedroom. "You're frightening me a little, Daniel."

"I'm frightening myself," he acknowledged lightly. "I may go into cardiac arrest." He jerked the bedclothes out of the way and sat down, pulling her in between his knees. "Let's both take a couple of deep breaths, okay? There. Better?"

She nodded, grinning. "Deep breathing, Haggarty? Is that your secret formula for sexual success?"

"Right now it's a last resort against sexual humilia-tion."

"You don't have to impress me." Having expected smooth sophistication, she was touched by his anxiety. She leaned over and kissed the top of his head. "Anything that happens is okay."

He smiled and kissed the soft flesh of her breasts. "You're too good to be true, you know that? Hush now. Don't talk anymore. Lie down."

He pulled her into bed and caressed her slowly from shoulder to thigh. She could feel his hands tremble as they explored her, and she knew she was trembling, too. Her palms trailed over his soft chest hair, tingling. His muscles rippled beneath her touch, and when she pressed her face to his chest, she heard the driving tempo of his heart.

He rolled her onto her back and threw a heavy thigh across her legs. "You like this?" He kissed her roughly, then tenderly, then roughly again. His hands moved on her pliant flesh, touching, smoothing, stroking, loving her everywhere.

"Mmm, yes." She shifted slightly, enjoying the feel of his weight upon her, his hard sinews against her softer, more yielding flesh. "Very much."

"Bret," he whispered. He kissed her throat and then her breasts, one after the other, sucking the rosy tips into his mouth and sighing with pleasure. "You taste like honey and flowers and wine."

Arching beneath him, she slid her hands down his naked back, kneading the hard muscles that shifted under her fingers. His teeth nipped her breasts, gently at first, harder as her excitement spiraled. First one, then the other, his tongue and teeth worshiped her breasts until she was crying out for his possession.

His fingers slipped lower, homing in on the source of her desire. She tossed her head back and forth on the pillow. He knew how to tease, how to touch, how to tune her to a fever pitch. Even though he was flushed with his own desire, even though his hands were shaking with restraint, he took his time about exciting her and giving her pleasure.

"My turn," she finally gasped, pushing at his shoulders until he rolled over onto his side. She wanted to please him as much as he was pleasing her. "Hold still a minute."

"I don't think I can."

"Don't argue." Reaching out, she found a nipple and rolled it between her finger and thumb. His growl of satisfaction pleased her. It made her feel powerful, and at the same time, very feminine.

"I love you to touch me," he admitted as her explorations continued. "Makes me feel wanted."

"Oh, you're wanted all right."

Her fingers walked over his tautened stomach, probed the hollow of his navel, hesitated momentarily, then sought the magnificent thrust of his manhood. He groaned as her light fingertips ventured along the shaft. He was throbbing, and she felt an answering series of spasms deep inside her.

"Nice," she told him, meeting his eyes with a mischievous smile. "When am I going to get it?"

"You witch, Bret." In a flash she found herself beneath him again, held immobile by his powerful body, his hard nakedness pressing insistently against the moist center of her passion. "Never tempt a starving man."

But he waited one more second, his hooded eyes asking for her permission. "Yes, for godsake, take me, take me, take me..." The words formed an urgent rhythm as their bodies slowly merged. Bret glowed with happiness because it felt so perfect, so right.

For a golden instant they were still, their eyes open and looking directly into each other's, and Bret felt all her defenses crumble. Smiling, she opened herself to him, body and soul. His hips plunged, and she met his

thrust with her own. Both cried out with the sheer pleasure of it. Her skin blossomed with the same dampness
it had known in the sauna as the heat inside her roared
into a conflagration. They drew apart, then joined again,
and she felt her soul spinning as the tension in her loins
wound ever tighter. Closing her eyes, she saw colors,
just as she had on the night they met—passionate blues,
steamy yellows, hot pinks, and scarlets.

Her hands slipped down over his tense body, exploring
him, reveling in his virile strength as he forced her into
a wild, haphazard rhythm. Holding him tightly, she let
herself go, trusting him to take her higher and higher
until her breathing grew shallow and her limbs started
to dissolve. There was one more moment of almost ag-
onizing pleasure before she slipped over the edge. She
was only vaguely aware of Daniel's hoarse cry as his
body went rigid with his own climax, but in the aftermath
they clung to each other, making small sounds of wonder
and awe at the extraordinary mutuality of their pleasure.

Afterward Bret's head rested on Daniel's shoulder,
his arms holding her body loosely, their legs tangled.
She was falling into a light slumber when she vaguely
heard him say, "Sleep, my love, my darling, my witchy
woman." His lips touched her eyelids tenderly. "Sleep."

Bret woke up sobbing. She'd seen Arthur in her
dreams, his limp body lying on the ground beside the
car, not moving while she strained to free herself from
the wreckage and smelled the ominous scent of gasoline.
Then he was beside the bed, lightly caressing her hair
and telling her he still loved her. "I'm alive," he said to
her. "Believe. Believe."

But when she opened her arms to him, he glared at
her with Daniel's eyes.

Then Daniel's voice was comforting her, saying, "Shh,
love, shh. It's okay. It was only a dream." His strong
arms enfolded her, and he lifted her atop him, his thighs

parting to imprison her between them. She felt his crinkly chest hair brushing against her breasts. "You were dreaming," he repeated.

"It was Arthur," she said shakily. "He told me to believe."

A fierce light sparked in Daniel's eye. "Believe what?" he demanded.

Bret rapidly pulled herself together. "Uh, nothing," she muttered, remembering that Daniel was the last person she could ever tell that she and Arthur had once lightheartedly agreed that whichever one of them died first would try to send the other a message from the Other Side—if the Other Side really existed. The message was to be the simple word *believe*. It would mean that somehow, somewhere, Arthur's spirit still survived. "I'm sorry. I must still be half asleep."

Daniel's voice was kind. "It's natural, Bret. Don't worry about it. It's the first time, and you feel a little guilty. It'll pass."

She heaved a sigh and buried her face in his shoulder. Although she tried to stifle them, the dream images still flitted across her mind. "I'm sure you're right," she whispered. "Hold me."

He held her tightly, and after a time he said, "Tell me about Arthur, Bret. You've been unusually loyal to him. He must have been really something."

"We practically grew up together," she answered slowly. "He lived down the street from me. We went steady in high school, and we ended up going to the same college. He was my first lover—my only lover . . . until tonight. We were married the day after college graduation." Her voice dropped as she remembered the carefree pleasures of those happy days. "I guess we both always thought we'd be together forever. I couldn't believe it when he died. It didn't seem possible. It was as if I'd been severed from an essential part of myself."

Daniel muttered something under his breath.

"What did you say?"

"I was cursing. It's even worse than I thought. I suppose the guy was perfect, too? Handsome, great personality, terrific in bed?"

Actually, Daniel was a much more exciting lover than Arthur had ever been. Once again she felt a faint disloyalty to Arthur. She had thought their relationship so perfect, yet the first experience she'd had with another man had been so much more ecstatic than anything she'd known with her husband. It shook her a little. "He was a sweet, kind, gentle man," she returned testily. "He wasn't perfect, but who is? I loved him."

"How long were you married?" he asked tightly.

"Nearly four years."

"Why didn't you have children? From what you say, Arthur would have been a model father."

Bret's hands touched her empty belly in an instinctively protective gesture. She rolled off Daniel and curled up beside him. "We wanted children more than anything," she whispered. She was going to cry, dammit.

Daniel propped himself up on one elbow and frowned into her eyes. "And?" he prompted.

"We had just started trying when he died." To her horror she felt hot tears flowing down her cheeks. She turned her face into the pillow and wept while Daniel lowered his body over hers and silently comforted her.

"I'm sorry," he murmured against her ear when she was finally still. "I want to know you, to understand you, but the last thing I want is to hurt you, Bret. Any time I ask you a question that disturbs you, you're free to tell me to go straight to hell."

As it had several times before, his tenderness moved her. Because he seemed to be such a forceful, aggressive man who would think nothing of riding roughshod over everybody else's feelings, Bret still felt surprised when he offered her kindness and consideration. "Thank you, Daniel. You're really . . . very nice," she finished lamely.

He turned her over and passed his hand along her cheeks, brushing away the last remnants of her tears. "Very nice?" he repeated, his mouth curling up in a dangerous smile. "Is that the best you can manage?" A finger strolled across her lips, then slipped down to smooth over her throat and breasts. His legs captured hers, and she felt his body stir and harden with renewed desire. "Let's see if we can't find a more suitable adjective for what I am, for what we are together."

The husky promise in his voice incited a yearning deep inside her. When he kissed her she rocked her pelvis against his until he groaned and slid between her thighs.

"I want you again," he said.

"Me, too."

"This time I'll do a better job of it. The first time was too fast."

"I loved the first time, Daniel."

"You'll love the second time, too. I intend to impress the hell out of you." His voice was determined, almost harsh. "I'm going to give you something new to dream about, Bret."

He kept his promise. The Daniel who made love to her now was a different Daniel from the man who'd exploded in her arms two hours before. No longer trembling with his need for release, he courted her leisurely, showering her with devastating sensuality. She was dazzled. He knew exactly where to touch her to give her the most exquisite pleasure. He knew how fast, how hard. He knew when to tease, and when to satisfy. He even knew what made her shy, and how to overcome her inhibitions.

The first time he used only his hands and his mouth to lead her to the edge of ecstasy, to hold her there for endless golden seconds, and finally to hurl her over. Thinking herself replete, she curled up and tried to rest against him, only to discover that he had no intention of letting her stop. Once again he aroused her, patiently seeking out every pleasure point on her body, finding many in the process that she'd never been acquainted with before. She felt like a virgin again, being introduced to pleasures that were beyond her experience and almost beyond her imagination.

"Lie still," he ordered at one point.

"Why?" she gasped, barely able to obey.

"Just lie still and feel me loving you." He moved inside her with tantalizing slowness, withdrawing and coming back to her after a breath-stealing delay. "I want you to feel me staking my claim on you, Bret Kingsley. I want it to be very clear to you exactly how alive we both are."

When he began to retreat again, she clasped her arms tightly around his back and tried to prevent him, but he was inexorable. "Lie still," he repeated as her hips strained upward in protest. His hand slipped between their bodies, seeking out the throbbing center of her passion. "I'm going to heighten your pleasure."

On some deep level his domination of their lovemaking thrilled her. It was totally new to her, this wild feeling of helplessness. Panting, she obeyed him, fighting the almost irresistible urge to move and feeling his slightest touch in every cell. "Some slave," she complained huskily as he continued the delicious torment. "You've got our roles reversed."

He chuckled, but his voice maintained its gently aggressive edge. "Speaking of role-playing, my darling witch"—he moved deeply within her while she gritted her teeth in her effort to prevent her body from undulating wildly beneath him—"I haven't forgotten the way you deceived me. You're no more qualified to tell fortunes than I am."

"Well, maybe a little more," she objected. "I have powers that I've, uh, never really bothered to develop. They run in the female line of my family."

He muttered a skeptical expletive and thrust into her

with such force that she thought he must surely hurt her, but she felt no pain, only pleasure. "Dear God, Daniel!" She let out an involuntary moan. "You're driving me crazy! May I move now?"

"No."

But she could tell from his breathing that his own control was slipping, so she defied him and moved anyway. He didn't seem to mind. He whispered her name tenderly against her lips as he slid his hands beneath her, guiding her wildly into his rhythm. Together they rode the final surge to completion, neither controlling the other now, both of them equal in the face of a storm of passion whose powers were greater than anything either of them possessed alone.

Afterward, lying flung out on her back in pleasant exhaustion, she murmured, "Wow, I am impressed."

"So am I." He kissed her affectionately. "You're quite a woman, Bret."

"I've never been able to...I mean, twice in a row like that."

He chuckled. "You see what you've been missing? These are your golden years; you're approaching your sexual peak."

"And you're past yours," she teased him. "Don't men peak at nineteen or thereabouts? I should find myself a college student."

"No way, darling. You're mine now." His voice was fiercely possessive. "Be content; in me you've got the best of both worlds. Deprive me for a few days, and you get hotblooded lust; satisfy me, and you get slow, sensual seduction. What more could you want, you lucky woman?"

"Humility?" she suggested.

He rolled on top of her, laughing, and she hugged him, feeling deliriously happy. He was tough, tender, and playful, all in one. She nestled closer, reveling in the feel of his hard, sweat-slick body. What more could she want? His love, of course. How easy it would be to love him!

Bret stiffened as she realized the unruly direction of her thoughts. Love him, indeed! This was exactly what she'd feared, dammit. Spend the night with a man, and—bingo!—she was in love.

Careful, Bret. She warned herself not to get carried away just because she was enjoying the pleasures of sex after three years of abstinence. It would be crazy to fall for D. D. Haggarty, no matter how much he prattled about the *more* he supposedly wanted from her. He was a whirlwind—pure passion, pure energy. No doubt he would blow out of her life as swiftly as he had blown in.

"What're you thinking?"

"Scorpio lovers," she murmured, closing her eyes.

"I looked us up in an astrology book this morning," he confided. "You're right: We're a perfect match."

"Ah-ha, the skeptic's walls are beginning to crumble!" she whooped. "Next I'll have you going to table-tappings and reading your horoscope each day."

"Don't be absurd," he said fiercely before kissing her into silence.

Chapter

7

IT WAS STILL snowing when they woke up on Sunday morning. Bret called Paul Tiele from the phone beside Daniel's bed and was told that rehearsals had been canceled because of the storm. The entire city was paralyzed. Most of the roads hadn't been plowed.

"Be in here tomorrow morning at ten," Paul said grouchily. "I don't care if you have to ski to work, Kingsley. This is probably all you fault, your know. Quoting from the play."

Daniel scowled when she hung up the phone and repeated her director's words. "Superstitious jerk," he muttered. Then he grinned. "You got the day off, huh?"

She laughed, noting the lecherous gleam in his dark eyes. "I can't imagine what I'm going to do with my time."

Daniel promptly pounced. They rolled over once, wrestling playfully, before he trapped her against the headboard. The now-familiar melting heat washed through her with an intensity that made her groan and press herself into his firm, lean strength. "I don't believe this. I feel depraved."

"From deprived to depraved in one night's time," he laughed, kissing her.

Later in the day they went sledding. Daniel's home in Winchester was just across the road from a golf course, where there was a long, steep grade known to the neighborhood children as Suicide Hill.

"Homicide Hill, more likely," Bret grouched as Daniel bundled her in his arms and seated them both on a rickety sled he'd bribed away from a ten-year-old. "Do I already bore you so much that you're trying to break my neck?"

"Hush. You're going to love it."

She did. The rush of wind against her face, the sharp slivers of snow sprayed up by the sled's metal runners, the sight of the pale afternoon sun finally breaking through the stormclouds, the sheer thrill of the speed they built up as they tore down the hill, all had her screaming with delight. "Let's do it again!" she cried when they finally coasted to a stop at the bottom. "Come on, I'll race you back up to the top of the hill."

She beat him, too, but not by much.

"Jock," he said, grabbing her in front of about twenty laughing kids and kissing her soundly. "You cheated!"

"Just because I gave you a little push into a snowbank?"

"Not to mention pelting me with snowballs!"

She grinned. There was snow sticking to his hair and eyelashes from the one soft missile he'd taken directly in the face. He looked as exuberant and boyish as the children around them. "You love it, Daniel!" she crowed.

"Yeah, but wait till I get you home—you'll love that even more." Whispering, so the children wouldn't hear, he added a more specific threat.

"You'll have to catch me first!" Throwing herself down on the sled, she took off down the hill without him, while the children squealed with amusement at the crazy grown-ups' antics.

Late that afternoon they sat together in Daniel's elegant living room, drinking tea and munching English biscuits in front of a cheery fire, and talked about their lives. Bret told him about her parents' divorce and the long years during which she had been shuffled back and forth between her professor father in California and her crackpot mother in New York. "My father's house was sane and rational, with a place for everything and everything in its place. My mother's house was . . . well . . . you'd have had to see it to believe it, Daniel. And even then . . ." She stopped, helpless to describe her mother's house to D. D. Haggarty, professional skeptic and witch-hunter.

"What was it—haunted?" he asked with a disparaging laugh.

She gave up. "Tell me about yourself."

He elaborated on what he had told her about his parents the night before, explaining that his mother had been devoted to his father even though his father was totally wrapped up in his job. "He was a commodities broker, as lucky as he was skillful at predicting trends. But he was obsessed with it. He was only forty when he had a heart attack on the trading floor. He never even made it to the hospital."

"How old were you?" she asked gently.

"Eleven. I was broken-hearted, and my mother was devastated," he explained. "She'd loved him deeply, and she simply couldn't handle the shock of his death."

He sipped the last of his tea and leaned back with his head against the sofa cushions as he continued. "She used to talk out loud to him, the way I heard you speak to Arthur that first night. Only she did it constantly. She couldn't accept what had happened; she couldn't let him go."

Fine shivers threaded over Bret's skin as she began to sense where this was leading. A moment later her fears were confirmed.

"One day my mother was visited by a friend who was into spiritualism. The 'friend' convinced my mother that my father was still there, watching over her and taking an interest in her life. She suggested that there might even be a message waiting for her from the Other Side."

Oh, no, thought Bret. So that was why...

"My mother began attending weekly seances. Soon she was 'communicating' upon a weekly basis with my father. Miraculously, she seemed happier, more alive, as if her newfound belief in life after death had given her the strength to enjoy her own life again.

"Then one day she decided to take me to the seance. I had been in a couple of fights at school, and my 'father' apparently thought I needed a good scolding." He paused a moment, his voice bitter. "All sorts of weird things happened, and I was scared out of my wits. When a face vaguely resembling my father's materialized out of the darkness over the medium's shoulder, I was so terrified I tipped my chair over backward. Purely by accident I tripped the level that opened the wall panel where the projector was concealed. My 'father' disappeared, and the medium was so rattled that she fell out of her fake trance and started screaming obscenities at me."

Bret silently soothed him, surprised at the amount of resentment she felt toward the fake medium. It was people like that who gave her mother's profession a bad name. Iris Carter would have been angry, too.

"We went back there the next day with my uncle, who was an attorney. He forced the medium to admit she'd been pulling the wool over my mother's eyes for

months. There had been no 'messages' from my father.
It was all a hoax."

"Your poor mother. I'm sorry, Daniel."

"She went into a deep depression that lasted for months.
She was never really the same afterward. It was as if all
the life had been sucked out of her. She died two years
later, of cancer." One of his hands was tightly clasping
hers; the other clutched the arm of the sofa. "I've always
hated spiritualists."

"No one could blame you," she whispered. Two years
later. Daniel had been left an orphan at thirteen, she
realized, aching for him.

A minute went by, then two. Daniel's hand moved,
his fingers interlacing with hers. "When I met you I
thought you were one of them, and it tore me apart
because I knew I wanted you. I knew I had to have you."

"And I teased you by letting you believe it." She was
desolated at the idea of causing him pain. "I shouldn't
have done that. Forgive me."

He looked into her eyes, and the world narrowed to
include just the two of them. "Look at you. You're ten-
derhearted as hell, you know that? I'll bet you cry buckets
over sad books and movies."

She nodded.

His expression softened, and his own tenderhearted-
ness showed clearly in his dark eyes. "Bret..." He
stopped. She was nestled against him, her hands in his,
her face near his shoulder, her eyes locked with his.

"What?"

"I don't make commitments easily, but—"

She quickly withdrew one of her hands and stopped
him by placing her fingers on his mouth. "It's okay.
Don't say any more." She didn't want him to say things
he might regret later.

He smiled and kissed her fingers. His eyes searched
hers; then his hand slipped around to the back of her
head and tilted her face to his. They kissed sweetly,
without lust or urgency, and settled closer into each oth-

er's arms. After a few minutes she broke the comfortable silence between them. There was something else she had to know.

"The medium, Daniel," she began hesitantly.

"Yes?"

"She wasn't my mother, was she? I mean, she couldn't have been. My mother never used tricks or projectors. She never willfully deceived anyone or abused her gift."

He frowned. "Your mother's a fake like all the rest," he insisted. "But, no, she wasn't the one. Her name was Myra Kelley."

"Of course. The fake medium you exposed on your program." Viciously, she remembered, *Let my enemies beware* . . .

"I dealt with her," he said with the harshness that was just as much a part of Daniel Haggarty as the tenderness was. "But I won't really feel satisfied until I roast all the false witches of spiritualism." *Including your mother.* He didn't say the words, but Bret knew he was thinking them.

For a long time there was silence. Finally Bret said, "Do you really think all mediums are complete and utter frauds?"

His dark eyes narrowed. "Absolutely."

"But strange things happen to people sometimes, things that simply cannot be explained. And my mother, crackpot though she is, has some incredible powers." She abruptly recalled the way she herself had known Daniel's name on the night they'd met. "Sometimes I think I may have inherited a few of them."

"I knew it," he growled. "You're going to turn out to be a witch after all."

"You can't imagine what it was like to be a child in my mother's house. Listen to me, and try to understand. It was never a question of 'do you believe in ghosts'— some of my mother's best friends were ghosts! She'd go around talking to them half the time."

"She sounds psychotic to me."

"No, she's not psychotic." Bret looked earnestly into his face, trying her best to explain. "Oh, she's a little flaky, that's for sure, but she was never incapable of taking care of herself, or of me, or of running the house and coordinating all her nutty activities. Besides, Daniel—I know you're not going to believe this—the ghosts used to answer back."

"I suppose you talked to them, too?" he asked dryly.

"In a way. They rapped. Once for no, twice for yes. Codes for letters of the alphabet. You could carry on a conversation with them if you wanted to."

"Knee joints," Daniel said sagely.

"What?"

"Don't you know that the two sisters who started the spiritualist movement in this country admitted before they died that they'd made their mysterious rapping sounds by cracking their knee joints? Or maybe it was their toe joints."

"Daniel, we're talking loud noises here! Sometimes on the wall, sometimes on the ceiling, sometimes right out of thin air. And that's not all. You know about telekinesis—things moving around by themselves, defying the law of gravity? And teleportation—things moving through walls? Not to mention clairvoyance. My mother can predict all sorts of events. When I think about it, it gives me the creeps!"

Daniel stroked her hair with soothing fingers. "Poor kid. You must have been frightened out of your wits most of the time."

She shook her head. "Oddly enough, I wasn't. It seemed rather ordinary to me, actually. I thought everybody's mother practiced witchcraft and consorted with spirits."

"Lord, Bret, I wish I were getting this on tape. Why won't you let me interview your mother? I'll probably do it anyway, you know. This material is too good to miss."

"What do you mean, you'll do it anyway?" she flared. "You promised you wouldn't interview her without my permission."

"Your permission *or hers* was what I promised."

"Well, you won't get hers without mine," Bret said uneasily. The subject made her unaccountably nervous. Her mother on TV? It would be a disaster. Iris didn't possess an ounce of caution or common sense. She would answer all the interviewer's questions with complete honesty and directness, admitting that she communed with spirits long dead as freely as any normal person would admit to picking up the telephone and talking to a friend in another city. She'd come across sounding like a certifiable maniac!

"You'd better forget the idea, Daniel. She may be a little odd, but she's my mother, and I won't stand back and allow you to demean her. I've heard about the kind of thing you do on your show. You and your crusading minions would eat her alive."

Daniel's eyes were dancing wickedly. "You mean you're not going to introduce me to your mother, darling? But mothers usually adore me. I'm considered such a good catch."

She punched him gently on the shoulder and suggested a few choicer terms for what he was.

If Bret had expected Daniel's take-charge domination of her life to end when he returned her to her house on Sunday evening, she was soon proved to be mistaken. He phoned her from his home Sunday night, and from his office Monday morning, and Monday evening he showed up at the theater to watch her rehearse. It was the beginning of a pattern that continued all week. D. D. Haggarty didn't do anything halfheartedly. "I'm your lover now," he informed her calmly. "I fully intend to share your life."

They spent every night together. He would drop her off at home on his way to the TV station so she could feed Chester and play with the poor animal for a couple of hours before she reported to the theater. Evenings Daniel spent at rehearsals with her, usually bringing work of his own to do while she was busy. He worked energetically, giving his full attention to whatever it was that absorbed him. He had the ability to narrow his concentration totally, never noticing a thing around him except what he was doing at the time.

He made love the same way—energetically and totally absorbed, in her, in the experience, in the magic they wove between them.

At night, late, when Paul Tiele finally released the exhausted company, Daniel drove Bret home once more to check on Chester, and then on to his house in Winchester. One night they stayed in Cambridge because Bret was feeling guilty about the cat. "He's lonely," she explained as she cuddled the huge purring feline. "I've never left him alone so much before."

It was the only night they didn't make love. Daniel was so doped up on anti-cat-allergy medication that he fell asleep as soon as they got into bed.

In the morning he woke her from a deep sleep and took her in the fiercely exciting manner she was becoming accustomed to. When she cried out in ecstasy, Chester meowed worriedly at the door.

"It's all right, Chester," she called, wiping a swathe of sweat-damp dark hair out of Daniel's eyes. "He thinks you're hurting me."

There was a crash in the hall, which Bret recognized as a vase biting the dust under the influence of Chester's swatting tail. Daniel swore. "I'm going to drown that damn cat."

"You should be grateful to him," she laughed. "We

both got some sleep for a change."

His laughter was a low growl. "You mean I work you too hard, woman? These dissolute nights getting to be too much for you? Maybe you're just out of shape. I notice you haven't been leaping out of bed at dawn to go swimming lately."

"I stop for a swim on my way to work," she informed him haughtily. "You're the one who could use some exercise."

"I run four or five miles every day at lunchtime."

"I didn't know that." She was surprised because she already felt as though she knew everything about him.

"Thought you had an indolent layabout in bed with you, huh?" He bent his dark head and dabbed a rosy nipple with the tip of his tongue. "Maybe I'll just resign myself to being late to work this morning in order to prove my stamina."

"I thought you'd just proved it," she breathed. Incredibly, his ministrations were causing that familiar tightening in her recently satiated body.

"I'll just have to prove it again. We wouldn't want there to be any doubt in your mind, would we?"

She shook her head. With Daniel she had found out that she was capable of the repeating cycles of arousal she'd read about in woman's magazines but had always suspected of being mythical.

"I'd really like to interview your mother," Daniel said on Friday evening, the night of the final preview before the official opening of the play. They were in his car on the way to the theater, but obviously Daniel's mind was still on his work. "I'm going to do an entire hour's program on spiritualists, and I've lined up three seance-goers, the president of some international spiritualist society, and a photographer who shoots pictures of what he claims are ghosts. All I need now is a medium. Your mother's the most famous."

"I said no, Daniel."

"Come on, Bret. What are you afraid of? She seemed willing enough the one time I talked with her about it."

"There are plenty of other mediums you can use."

"I want Iris Carter. Long before I knew you, Bret, I intended to use her for the show. She's the best. Exposing her as a fraud would present the greatest challenge."

Bret's countenance darkened with anger. "Is that the way you regard attacking somebody on the air in front of thousands of people—as a challenge? You're talking about my *mother,* Daniel!"

He shrugged. "Maybe I'd fail. If she really has as much power as you claim she has, why do you fear for her? Maybe she'll turn my interviewer into a bat."

"Very funny."

"I want her, Bret."

"Then choose between us, Haggarty. Because I promise you, the day you go after my mother will be the day I break off our relationship."

Daniel pulled into a tiny parking lot behind the theater and shot her an ominous look. "You really think you still have that option? That you can simply walk away? No, Bret." His voice was soft, deceptively mild. "Things have gone too far between us for that."

She could feel the aura of masculine power he projected. Every now and then he still reminded her of the malevolent-looking devil he'd been on the night they first met. "I don't know what you mean," she said stubbornly.

"Think about it," he suggested as they stepped out into the cold. "If you're still in doubt later tonight, I'll he happy to demonstrate exactly what I mean."

She thought about his statement several times during the course of the evening. *Things have gone too far between us.* What did he mean? She knew he wasn't in love with her. As passionate as his lovemaking was, he'd made no further attempt to say the words that would confirm a growing emotional bond. He'd told her he could make her no promises, and she'd accepted that.

But her own feelings for him grew exponentially with every minute she spent at his side. The more she learned about him, the more he seemed to typify everything a man should be: strong, yet gentle; aggressive, yet kind; serious in all his purposes, yet blessed with the gift of laughter. She'd stopped comparing him to Arthur. She hadn't even thought about Arthur in days.

She daydreamed about Daniel when he wasn't with her, and she chattered about him to her friends in the cast until they all began to tease her about the new love in her life. All of them except Graham.

"Scorpio," he'd been muttering all week long. "Wait till you feel the slash of the deadly scorpion's tail. Don't cross him, Bret, or he'll turn on you for sure."

She'd scoffed at Graham's predictions, but she shivered.

Graham played on her anxieties a little more Friday night after the play. Daniel had disappeared for a few minutes to make a phone call, and Graham snatched the opportunity to say, "Of all the men to pick, Bret—why him? I watched *Facts and Fantasy* the other night. They were doing a thing on child abuse. I never thought I'd feel sorry for a child abuser, but by the time D. D. Haggarty's vultures had finished with her, I actually wanted to comfort the poor woman. The people they interview on that show take more punishment than the bad guys at the end of a cop show."

"I've never seen the program," Bret confessed. It was shown on Wednesday evenings, and she was always working.

"I had a friend record it for me," Graham said. "I want you to come over and watch it one of these days. It'll be quite a revelation. Is he still hunting witches, by the way? I hope you haven't given him any dazzling demonstrations of your psychic talents lately, luv."

"My psychic talents, if I have any, are not the stuff TV exposés are made of."

"I don't trust him. Maybe I'm clucking over you like some bloody mother hen, but I have a gut feeling he's going to hurt you. I still don't understand why you fell for him. You loved Arthur, and he was so . . . safe."

"*Safe* is boring!" she burst out. "I mean—" She stopped, flustered.

Graham was staring even more intently.

"Were you bored with Arthur? You mean there were problems with your marriage?"

"No, no, there weren't any problems. Arthur and I were very happy. It's just that he wasn't as—as exciting as Daniel. He was so passive." She struggled a little as she tried to verbalize feelings she didn't entirely understand. "We never even fought over anything. Don't you think that's a little strange, Graham? I mean, he was so perfect!"

"I can see why he might seem perfect in comparison with D. D. Haggarty," Graham began. Then, looking over Bret's shoulder, he abruptly broke off.

"Who might seem perfect in comparison with me?" said a low, dangerous voice from the doorway.

Bret bit her lip as she turned to face Daniel. "That was a quick phone call."

He came in, his hands thrust into the pockets of his jeans making fists that bulged the already tight material. He looked from her to Graham and back. "Who's this paragon of perfection you're comparing to me?"

"Nobody." "Arthur." Bret and Graham spoke simultaneously. Bret immediately turned to glare at Graham. She had learned that Daniel didn't care to hear references to her dead husband.

"Oh, *Arthur*," said Daniel emphatically, scowling at Bret. "We all know that nobody could ever hope to measure up to Arthur."

Bret quietly put on her coat. It had been more and more evident all week that Daniel and Graham could barely tolerate each other, and she didn't want to see the situation degenerate into total war. "I'm ready, Daniel. Let's go."

"Show a little caution for the rest of the night, Bret," Graham advised. "Venus is moving into opposition with Mars, and as for your planet, Neptune—"

"We're not interested in that drivel," Daniel snapped.

"Excuse me. The voice of reason speaks. When are you going to have a priest on your program, Haggarty, so you can mock his silly belief in the existence of God?"

"I might decide to go after an astrologer or two first," Daniel shot back. "How would you like some TV exposure, Hamilton? Or are you afraid some big Hollywood talent scout might see you make a fool of yourself?"

"If astrology is such drivel, I wonder why it describes your personality so accurately. I also wonder why you're pursuing Bret. You know her background; she's her mother's daughter. What are you going to do if she goes into a trance on you someday? Film it for your viewers' amusement?"

Daniel stared at him without answering, but Bret said angrily, "I don't go into trances—just rages. And right now it'll only take one more word from either of you to set me off."

Graham paid no attention. "You're not her type, Haggarty," he plunged on. "And, frankly, I can't imagine how a woman who was happy with a warm, gentle man like Arthur Kingsley could long put up with a witch-hunting devil like you."

Bret shivered as Daniel reached out and seized her hand in one of his. His palm was damp with nervous tension. He was vibrating with it. He was so explosive, it frightened her sometimes.

"She knew what I was from the start," Daniel said, as much to her as to Graham. "I've always been honest with her. She knew the risks, and she took me anyway. Now she's stuck with me."

Bret tried to free her hand. "Will you let go of me, dammit?"

"Never," he answered darkly, pushing her toward the door.

"You're all wrong for her, you know," Graham called after them. "You'll lose her, coming on like a bloody warlord."

Daniel thanked him ironically for the advice.

They drove home in almost total silence. Bret was fuming, and Daniel operated the car in a jerky fashion, his hands hard on the wheel, his foot pounding the clutch. When they got to her house Bret slammed inside and cuddled Chester, pressing her face into his thick orange fur and telling herself that her life would have been a lot less complicated if she'd followed her first instinct and run away from D. D. Haggarty the moment she met him.

Daniel followed her in and stood watching her, his eyes gleaming beneath his thick black lashes. Chester was purring and kneading her forearm. "Poor baby," she soothed the neglected cat. "Did you miss me?"

Looking up at Daniel, she said, "I'm staying with my cat tonight. It's cruel to leave him alone so much."

Daniel reached out and scratched Chester's head. "You'd better start giving that some thought. I'm fond of the beast, but I can't live with him. Chester's going to need a new home."

Bret felt as if he'd kicked her in the gut. She gathered Chester even more tightly against her. "What do you mean?" she flared. "You're not going to separate me from everyone I love—my friends, my cat . . ." *My mother,* she was thinking.

He shook his head, his eyelashes flicking up and down over his burning eyes. Once again she felt the tension in him. Any minute he would go off like a firecracker. "I don't want to argue. Get your things. You're coming with me."

Her eyes narrowed, and her nostrils flared. "Or what?" she challenged. "You'll get primitive and club me over the head, caveman?"

He reached out and negligently stroked the side of her neck, much the same way she was stroking Chester. An involuntary shiver took her, and her lips parted slightly. As always, his electric effect on her body was devastating "This thing between us *is* primitive," he said quietly. "You know damn well neither one of us can resist it, no matter how angry we get with each other." After a brief silence he added, "I'm sorry for arguing with Graham. I don't know why I let him get to me. I'll try not to do it again."

Sighing, Bret put the cat down and opened the door to let him out. She hadn't expected Daniel to apologize. "It's beyond me why you get so uptight every time Arthur's name is mentioned. You think about him more than I do!"

"Nobody likes being compared with a saint."

"I wasn't comparing you. Graham was."

"He doesn't like me. He's trying to make trouble between us."

"Don't blame Graham for that," she said tightly, recalling their earlier argument about her mother. "We seem to be able to fight perfectly well without outside interference."

He ran a hand through his hair and seemed, momentarily, to be fumbling for words. "Look, Bret, there wouldn't be any trouble if you just relaxed and accepted the inevitable." He moved closer, drawing her against the warm sinews of his body. "There's something very powerful between us. And no one—not your mother, not Arthur, not Graham—is ever going to be able to interfere with that."

Bret's head ached slightly. She didn't know whether

to be pleased or annoyed by his words. He had her off-balance. With all her feminine instincts she could sense his masculine arousal, his desire to possess her in the most ancient, basic way. But, as she'd told him from the start, she needed more.

"What do you want from me, Daniel?" She deliberately moved her hips against his. "Just this? You have my body. Does it satisfy you?"

"I love your body," he said with a sudden devastating smile, "but now I want your soul."

"You're beginning to sound like the devil you resemble."

He shot a glance at himself in the hallway mirror. "I resemble the devil?"

"Not all the time," she qualified. Remarkably, the mood had subtly lightened. "Let's just say you have your moments of deviltry."

He grinned and hooked his hands on her shoulders, drawing her closer. His heat shot through her, sparking her from head to toe. His head lowered, his tongue washed over her lips, preparing them for his kiss. "As you have your moment of witchcraft. It's very appropriate, you know. One of the attributes of witches is that they consort with the prince of darkness. Want to consort, sorceress?"

She laughed and leaned into his chest. She couldn't help herself; he was irresistible. "Your place or mine?"

He sneezed, and the matter was decided.

When they entered his house a little while later Daniel took her straight up to the bedroom. She recognized the glow in his eyes, and it sent her body leaping into glorious arousal.

"Get undressed," he ordered, his voice harsh and gravelly.

She felt a primordial feminine desire to tease him. She removed her clothes with maddening slowness, her eyes never leaving his. Her blouse had a prim line of tiny buttons down the front, and she painstakingly undid every single one while he stood stiffly facing her, a flush of barely contained excitement evident over the hard bones of his face. When she slid sensuously out of her colorful peasant skirt, she noticed that he was breathing rapidly through parted lips. Knowing she had the power to arouse him so completely thrilled her. It also made her flirt, a little, with danger.

She removed her sheer panty hose, then approached him wearing only a delicate black bra and matching bikini. "What about you?" she said huskily. She tunneled a hand under his sweater, finding the pelt of hair on his abdomen and curling her fingers into it. Her bare legs brushed against his trousers while her fingers fumbled with his belt. Her green eyes met his mischievously. "I want to see your body, too." The hand that was under his sweater found a nipple and sensuously toyed with it. The other hand slipped inside his loosened trousers and captured the hard thrust of his maleness, making him groan.

The next thing she knew the room was arcing around her as Daniel swooped her up in his arms and carried her to the bed. He fell on her, clothes and all, and after a few rapid fumblings with her bikinis and his trousers, they were naked from the waist down. She could feel his body tremble as he lowered his full weight upon her and parted her thighs. The wool sweater he still wore was faintly rough against her lace-covered breasts. They made no move to finish undressing; there was something fiercely exciting in their mutual urgency to complete the union.

"I'll teach you to taunt me," he growled, closing his mouth over hers. His hips drove against her, and she arched to accommodate him, sighing with pleasure as he sank into the warm folds of her body, filling her emptiness exquisitely.

"I wasn't taunting you," she gasped. She had wrapped her arms around his back, under the sweater. She could feel the driving tension of the muscles that bunched and relaxed as he began to move within her.

"You're mine," he muttered. "Forever and ever. I want to hear you say it, witch." One of his hands slid between their bodies to tantalize a budding nipple through the fabric of her bra. Simultaneously he slowed the rhythm of their loving until he was barely moving. He ignored the way her body strained for a quick, violent conclusion.

"Daniel!" she cried in protest as he abruptly withdrew. A quick look at his taut expression told her he had somehow marshalled the strength to control his passion. Supporting his weight on his strong arms, he slid himself back and forth between her thighs and watched her in narrow-eyed satisfaction as she pleaded for him to forge their union anew.

"Say it," he repeated. There was a sheen of perspiration on his brow, and Bret knew he couldn't keep this up much longer. "Admit that you belong to me." His head dipped to tongue an aching, lace-clad nipple. The exquisite friction made her sob with desire.

"I'm yours, dammit!" she moaned, pulling furiously at his shoulders.

He made a noise that probably would have been an exultant laugh if he hadn't been so close to the limits of his willpower. But he still didn't take her until, incensed, she reached down and fondled him intimately. He surrendered to her then, driving raggedly into her yielding body, taking her higher and higher until she felt shards of pleasure piercing her and the explosive burst of glory that made their spirits one. Dimly, in the aftermath, she heard herself saying, "Yes, yes, I love you, I love you Daniel. I'm yours for as long as you want me."

His mouth met hers, and she felt him smile in satisfaction, but he made no answer.

She dreamed that night that he had stalked and hunted her and that now he was erecting bars around her, caging her. Little by little the witch-hunter was making his predatory nature felt.

Chapter

8

WHEN BRET OPENED her eyes the following morning she found Daniel already awake, propped up on one elbow, watching her. Memories of the night flooded her, making the color rise in her cheeks. He smiled slightly and brushed a lock of raven hair out of her eyes.

"Morning, sweetheart," he said. His voice was husky with unmistakable male satisfaction.

"What are you smirking about?"

Suddenly he was all little-boy innocence. "Smirking? Me?"

"You look the way I'd imagine Chester would look if he ever actually caught one of the birds he's always chasing."

"Poor Chester. He's too fat and clumsy ever to catch anything." He ran a finger down the side of her throat. "I'm a much better hunter than he is."

Bret was astonished at the resentment that flashed through her. He looked so pleased with himself—oh, didn't he just! She rolled away from him, threw back the covers, and got up.

"Where are you going? It's Saturday. We can stay in bed."

"I don't feel like staying in bed." She jerked open the curtains and let the sunshine into the room. "I feel like getting up and being active."

"If it's exercise you want—" he began suggestively, but he broke off when he saw the way she was glaring at him. His expression changed instantly, becoming wary, even a little concerned. "Bret? What's the matter?"

What's the matter? I told you I loved you last night, that's what's the matter. And you didn't even acknowledge my words.

"Nothing."

"Then come back to bed."

"No thanks." She grabbed her clothes, walked into his bathroom, and shut the door.

She half expected him to come storming in after her, but, as usual, Daniel surprised her. When she returned, washed and dressed for the day, Daniel was sprawled out across the bed, sound asleep. "You're pretty damn sure of yourself, aren't you, Haggarty?" she said out loud.

Again he didn't respond.

The play officially opened that evening, and Bret was more nervous than usual. Her affair with Daniel had been preying on her mind all day long. Insensitive clod! Couldn't he see how important he'd become to her? Didn't he feel anything in return for her besides typical male possessiveness? She was tempted to challenge him on the issue but feared that if she did, he'd only repeat what he'd started to tell her earlier about his difficulty in making commitments.

He'd promised to be at the opening that night, and by the time eight o'clock rolled around, Bret's anxiety about her love life had transformed itself into a bad case of stage fright.

"I keep feeling as if something awful's going to happen," she told Graham backstage.

For once Graham didn't say anything about the position of her stars. He simply gave her a hug and pushed her out onstage.

Her fears seemed to have been unfounded, however. *Macbeth* went off more smoothly than ever, and the audience was warmly enthusiastic. By the time the final curtain fell, Bret's gloom had vanished and she, along with everyone else in the cast, began to share the heady feeling of having successfully accomplished exactly what they'd set out to do.

The cast and their friends, including Daniel, were milling about toasting each other backstage after the performance when Graham called Bret from the backstage door.

"Bret, luv, there's somebody from the audience who wants to congratulate you," he told her. Bret turned . . . and saw her mother.

"Mum!" she cried, staring at the small, white-haired woman decorously clinging to Graham's arm. Oh, no! She wondered if this was the something awful she'd been dreading. Daniel had gone stiff and silent at her side. The confrontation she'd been trying to avoid was upon them.

Blinking in dismay, Bret ran to throw her arms around her mother. "What are you doing here?"

"I came to watch your performance, of course," her mother answered placidly. "I didn't want to tell you beforehand, in case it made you nervous."

"But how did you get here?"

"I took a taxi," Iris said proudly, as if taking a taxi were a marvelous feat. For her mother, Bret reflected wryly, it probably was. She lived only two towns away, but she usually stuck close to home, letting Bret come to her. "You were good, but Bret, really, the spell doesn't go quite like that, you know. You got several of the exhortations wrong."

Bret was very conscious of Daniel hovering over them, listening to every word. She laughed nervously. "I said it the way Shakespeare wrote it, Mum; that's what they pay me for. Good heavens, this is such a surprise!" *I wish you'd warned me.* "Come in and meet everybody."

Daniel, naturally, was the first to demand an introduction. He bowed in a courtly fashion and took Iris's hand as if he meant to kiss it. "I've been looking forward to meeting you for a long time, Mrs. Carter."

"Really, young man?" Iris looked him over. "You're not a member of the acting company, are you?"

"This is Daniel, Mother. A friend of mine."

Iris smiled a little vacantly as her spooky blue eyes wandered again over Daniel. "Ah, yes, Daniel. Something to do with television, wasn't it?"

"We spoke on the phone," he confirmed. "About doing an interview."

"Oh, yes. Bret told me some most uncomplimentary things about you, Daniel," Iris said with her usual unblinking honesty. "I must say I'm surprised you and she are still friends."

"We're very close friends as a matter of fact."

Iris's smile grew warmer. "Really? Then perhaps you're the one I've been expecting. You took your time about it, didn't you? My daughter has been alone far too long."

Daniel raised his eyebrows at Bret as he answered, "I intend to see that she's alone no longer."

Iris was beaming now. "Such an authoritative tone. Scorpio, of course." She sighed. "These are the times when I do so wish Bret had a strong father who would stand beside her and demand to know whether or not your intentions are honorable." She paused. "But, of course, you and I know the answer to that, don't we, Daniel?" She peered directly into his eyes as, for a few instants, a battle of wills seemed to flare between them. Then Daniel broke eye contact, looking at Bret with a faint expression of shock.

"Willful and stubborn," Iris chided him. "You guard your mind well, but you are curious, Daniel, aren't you? The drive to know the truth is stronger than your prejudice. Can you feel yourself changing? Loosening up? Becoming a little more open-minded?"

"Mother..." Bret interrupted. Daniel's face was flushed, and for the first time since she'd known him, Bret saw him at a total loss for words. She herself didn't know whether to laugh or slink away in embarrassment. A few years before, embarrassment would have won out, but recently Bret had stopped feeling so defensive about her mother. Once she had longed for the ordinary sort of mother everybody else had, but now she was almost proud to be the daughter of such an original.

Still, Daniel was the last person she wanted her mother to exercise her powers on. It wouldn't take much to incite him. Poor Iris had no idea what she was up against.

"Don't narrow your devil-black eyes at me, young man. I'm far too old to be intimidated in that manner," Iris went on blithely. Smiling, she turned back to Bret. "Good for you, my dear. It's about time you chose a man with spirit."

"Don't say anything," Bret hissed at Daniel a few minutes later as they stood together watching Iris chat animatedly with Paul Tiele.

"Who's saying anything?"

"I told you she was, uh, different."

"She's different all right." He was still flushed and tense. "She tried some kind of weird mind-trick on me. She's lucky she wasn't born in an earlier century."

"It's lucky we all weren't. You'd have been the first

to demand the witches' execution if you'd lived back then."

He shrugged. "You may be right. I suppose a TV program like mine is about the closest this society comes to public execution." His gaze flicked thoughtfully over her mother as he added, "Damn. I wish I had a camera crew here tonight. Maybe if I called the station—"

"Forget it, Daniel."

"You led me to believe she was foggy-brained and tottering on the brink of the grave."

"I did not. I said she was retired and that she didn't do interviews."

"I don't know why you're so overly protective of the woman. It's evident she can fend for herself."

"She's my mother, Daniel," Bret said hotly. "I repeat, if you ever so much as point a microphone in her direction, I'll never speak to you again."

Daniel glared at her in irritation for a second before his features slowly relaxed into a smile. "Don't make promises you can't keep," he said maddeningly. "You've got yourself a man with spirit this time, remember?"

How could she forget? A flashback of last night's lovemaking assaulted her, making her fingernails bite into her palms. Once again she remembered the words he'd wrung out of her—words of love, words of commitment. And from him? Nothing.

Maybe she should break things off with him. Maybe she should turn her back and run before she sank without a trace into the heartless pit he had dug for her soul. The dark lord of the underworld...

"Bret?" His fingers traced over her cheeks. "What's the matter?"

She shook herself. "Not a thing," she said brightly. "Did somebody mention a party?"

Somebody had. Graham was inviting everyone in the cast over to his place for an impromptu celebration. And his summons had already been accepted by Iris, who announced happily that she hadn't been to a party in years. "Aren't you tired, Mother?" Bret objected. "Why don't I just take you home?"

"No, no. Dear Graham has a psychic friend he's going to introduce me to. He's already offered me a ride, and I've accepted." She looked at Daniel, who was frowning. "But if you and your young man are tired, my dear, why don't you go along home? Don't think about me. Perhaps I'll spend the night at Graham's apartment if it gets too late."

"Of course," Graham said smoothly. He and Bret's mother were old buddies, and Bret knew he was fond of Iris. "My guest room is at your disposal." And without allowing Bret to say anything more on the matter, he bundled Iris off into his car.

"I think we should go home," she told Daniel as they got into the Porsche in back of the theater.

"Don't be absurd. We're going to Graham's party."

His peremptory tone annoyed her. "I thought you couldn't stand Graham."

"Surely you're not going to abandon your mother at this hour of the night."

"My mother understands that I want to be alone with you."

He flashed her a leer. "We'll have plenty of time to be alone later."

"You're hot on my mother's trail, aren't you, witch-hunter? Can't bear to let the quarry out of your sight. Have you ordered a camera crew to meet us at Graham's apartment?"

He glowered at her, not answering, following the car in front of them toward Graham's Boston apartment. Bret fumed in silence. D. D. Haggarty would do whatever the hell he wanted, of course. He always did.

At the party Bret was so angry with Daniel that she spent the next half hour avoiding him. He didn't seem to notice; he was too busy hanging around her mother.

Bret didn't tune into the general discussion until she heard somebody mention the infamous curse on *Macbeth*. "Maybe Iris can help us get to the bottom of that superstition," Graham suggested. "She knows all about spirits and witches and things."

Uh-oh, thought Bret, noting the way her mother snapped to attention and demanded an explanation. She also noted the devious look Graham directed at Daniel. Graham was still resentful about their argument last night, she realized. She wouldn't put it past him to turn the party into a forum on superstition and psychic phenomena just to annoy the skeptic among them.

"I've heard that there's an actual witches' spell in Act Four," said Paul Tiele. "One theory has it that the evil spirits called up by the spell must wreak some havoc before they're allowed to return to wherever it is they came from."

"There is a witches' spell in the play," Iris confirmed. "But it's worded incorrectly, so I doubt it would call up any spirits. On the other hand," she went on after pausing for thought, "some of the darker spirits are notoriously devilish. Perhaps one of them has a particular aversion to the incantation used in the play. He may even have been offended by the playwright, either here or in the Other World."

"Offended by the playwright?" Daniel repeated in a low, sarcastic tone. He had edged around the guests and was now standing just behind Bret, his fingers lazily massaging the nape of her neck.

"Shut up."

"My kingdom for a camera crew."

"It would be nice to know exactly what it is that brings down the ill fortune," Paul mused. "This play's got several weeks to run, followed by additional performances in repertory. I'd very much like to avoid disasters."

"Why don't we summon the spirits and ask?" Graham suggested. "We've got a famous medium here, after all.

We could hold a seance. How about it, Iris, are you up to it?" he added with an unmistakably malicious glance at Daniel.

"I could attempt it, of course. One never knows, though, I must warn you. The spirits do not always come at the beck and call of those of us who are still in the fleshly realm."

"Oh, dear God," moaned Bret. She glared at Graham, who blithely ignored her. "Really, Mother, don't you think it's much too late at night for that sort of thing? I'm exhausted. Daniel and I were just about to leave."

"Run along, then, dear. I've decided to stay with Graham tonight anyway. I'll talk to you tomorrow."

"Mother!"

Bret subsided at the touch of Daniel's hand on her arm. "Leave her alone," he ordered. "If she wants to do it, let her."

She turned to look at his face, but Daniel's attention was on Iris. Bret recognized his expression. It was the same one he had worn on the night they first met, when he looked into her eyes and threatened to burn her. "Oh, criminy, let's get out of here."

Daniel's eyes were gleaming beneath his thick lashes. "And leave your poor mother to the mercy of these characters? No, let's just consider it research for my project on spiritualism."

The bad feeling that had been bothering Bret on and off all day returned in full force. The last thing she wanted was a confrontation between her mother and Daniel on this very explosive issue. "Please, Daniel, you hate spiritualists. You don't want to witness my mother doing a seance, for godsake."

"On the contrary." He smiled grimly. "I can think of few things I'd rather witness." And he refused to budge.

While chairs were being arranged in a circle in the living room, Bret tried again. "I'm going to wait outside."

Daniel's fingers closed around her wrist. "No, you're not. You're damn well going to stay until the game is played out."

For a moment Bret felt it might actually be possible to hate D. D. Haggarty. But the feeling swiftly changed to self-disgust. His thumb was rubbing sensuously over the pulse point on her wrist, while his entire attention was on Iris. She doubted he was even conscious of the tiny massage he was giving her or of the shivers of desire it aroused within her.

She was angry, yet he could arouse her sexually without even being aware of it! Lord, she was really hooked. Enslaved, she corrected herself, staring at the fingers that enclosed her wrist like a manacle. Just as she'd feared, she was out of her depth in this relationship. She had been from the start.

Depression settled over her. She was going to have to end it, she thought in misery. He was breaking her.

When the seance began Bret sat as far away from her mother as possible. Daniel took the seat beside her, with Paul Tiele on her other side. Paul was chattering nervously, but Daniel was silent, watching the medium's preparations. These were simple enough, Bret was glad to see. Iris Carter did not require a special table, a particular position with respect to doors and windows, or even a completely darkened room.

She sat in a comfortable chair within the circle of guests, closing her eyes and relaxing her thin, birdlike body. She gently requested that they join hands to form a circle, then, without giving further instructions, she retreated into silence.

"What's she doing?" Daniel demanded after several minutes passed uneventfully. "Meditating?"

"Something like that. She's emptying her mind and body so she'll be able to receive whatever messages the spirits wish to send through her."

"Has she got a spirit control who guides the 'dear departed' to her?"

"Yes, of course. His name is Sir Geoffrey Vernon. He's an eighteenth-century British squire. A friend of Samuel Johnson's, I believe. He reported once that Sam was delighted to find out there was a life beyond. Apparently his faith wavered greatly during his sojourn on earth."

Daniel muttered something under his breath.

"You insisted on staying, so spare me your scoffing."

Almost immediately thereafter a convulsion shook Iris's body, and the muscles in her face altered in an eerie fashion, changing her appearance dramatically. One of the woman in the circle let out a small cry of alarm, and somebody else shushed her. "Good day to you," said a hollow-sounding male voice from Iris's throat. "For what purpose am I thus summoned?"

Daniel made another disapproving sound, which Bret endeavored to ignore. She, as always, was a little awed at her mother's strange transformation. Far better than Daniel, she was aware that "Sir Geoffrey Vernon" knew things Iris had never had access to. He spoke with a polished British accent, using words and idioms that had been current in the 1700s, and he was almost completely ignorant of the conventions of modern life. Bret had heard theories suggesting that Vernon and other spirit controls like him were actually submerged aspects of the medium's own personality. It was possible, she supposed. She had never known exactly what to make of him.

"Who's going to talk to him?" Paul Tiele whispered. His face was white, and he was holding Bret's other hand nearly hard enough to cut off her circulation. "She's your mother, Kingsley. Say something."

Bret shook her head. There was no way she was going to involve herself in this. She glared at Graham. This had been his clever idea; let him do it.

Graham was looking a little peaked himself. He ran his tongue nervously over his lips and said, "Who are you?"

In a dry voice Vernon identified himself, adding, "And who, might I ask, are you?"

"I'm, uh, Graham Hamilton, an astrologer," declared Graham in an obvious attempt to jump on the psychic bandwagon.

Through Iris, Vernon snorted loudly. "Fiddlesticks! All astrologers are charlatans, the buggers! I' faith, I've no wish to speak with one."

Graham was momentarily speechless, but Bret could feel Daniel chuckling. "Your mother has quite a sense of humor."

"Be quiet," she whispered.

Instead, Daniel raised his voice. "Will you speak to a man who hates charlatans as much as you do?" he asked the medium. "A rationalist who doesn't accept the existence of ghosts?"

Iris looked in Daniel's direction, and Bret shivered slightly. She would have been willing to swear on the Bible that the intelligence staring out of her mother's eyes bore not the faintest resemblance to sweet, flaky Iris Carter.

"I' faith, why not?" responded Vernon. "Verily enough I was a rationalist myself, in life. What would you ask of me?"

"Ask him about the play," Paul Tiele prompted.

"I myself would ask you for details about the so-called Other Side, but—"

"I' truth, I am not at liberty to divulge them," interrupted Vernon.

"I suspected as much," Daniel said smoothly. "The other people present are curious about a supposed curse on the play *Macbeth* and wish to contact someone who can set their minds at ease."

"You're not supposed to name the play," Tiele complained. "It calls down the curse."

"Did you hear that, Sir Geoffrey? You address a group of actors who are shaken with superstitious fear."

Iris's head turned as Vernon examined the faces of those present. "Scurvy lot," he said dismissively. "Never cared for actors myself. Although Davy Garrick, now, there's a fine a tragedian as ever walked the boards. Shall I look for Davy and ask him if he ever feared such a curse?"

"I thought we might ask old Will Shakespeare himself if he'd ever willfully offended any demons," Daniel suggested so sarcastically that Paul Tiele was moved to object.

"If you're not going to take this seriously, Haggarty, why don't you leave the circle?"

"Now, Shakespeare, there's a rollicking fine fellow," said Sir Geoffrey Vernon. "Never read 'im myself, o' course, but Johnson says—" He stopped abruptly, and Iris's head fell forward. Bret tensed—these sessions were a strain on her mother, and she was no longer young and strong—but almost immediately Iris raised her head again, and Vernon said in a different tone, "Wait. There's someone here. There's . . . i' faith, I cannot tell exactly. Aye. A most determined young man. What?" Vernon looked inward, speaking not to the group, it seemed, but to someone—or something—they could not see. "Wait. I will inquire. A young man is here," he said, addressing Daniel again. "Seeking his wife. He has something to tell her, he says. Quite concerned about it he is, too. What? Something about bread? A crust of bread? No? Oh, *Bret*. Is there a woman here called Bret? Damn fool of a name, I might add."

Bret cleared her throat, telling herself that her mother must be in a genuine trance, or how could she ask such a question? Daniel's fingers were crushing the bones in her hand. She couldn't tell if he was trying to be reassuring or if he was about to blow his top.

"Have you forgotten me, Sir Geoffrey?" she asked. "There was a time when you and I were pretty good friends."

But the spirit was apparently immune to sarcasm. "Bret? Good. I have a message for you from"—there was a pause; then the medium continued with slight questioning intonation—"from King Arthur."

Somebody giggled. Daniel distinctly muttered a curse, and somebody said, "Shh!" Bret felt her lover's body shift as if he were going to jump up and put an end to this, so she resolutely kicked him in the shin. "It's dangerous to the medium to interrupt in the middle of a sitting," she hissed at him. "You asked for this; now accept the consequences."

He was tense as a board, but he didn't interrupt. Bret turned back to Sir Geoffrey. "King Arthur? Are you sure that's his name?"

There was another long pause. "Kingsley, Arthur. Arthur Kingsley. Are you acquainted with a young man named Arthur Kingsley?"

"I might be," Bret replied. She ordered herself to stay calm. It's not really Arthur she told herself. It's just my mother, doing something she's done a thousand times before.

"It's Arthur," the control rasped. "He cannot stay. He's going back. He only wants to say . . . what? I cannot hear you, lad. What? Danger?" There was a short silence, and Bret tried to ignore the way her heart was throbbing. "He begs that you be wary of . . . what? Beware the fire."

"Beware the fire?" Bret repeated, her mouth dry.

"It will burn you," the hollow voice continued, more loudly now. "Take no risks. Do not try to salvage your heart from the ashes. The heat is too strong."

Bret shivered and withdrew her hand from Daniel's. Since the night she had met him, the image of fire had symbolized Daniel and the passion between them. "Is that all?" she asked shakily. Daniel seized her hand again, holding it fiercely in a grip she could not break. His palm was hot and moist—a telltale signal of his agitation.

"He also says...No. No. He must go. He has one more message for you though. Believe, he says. He's repeating the word *believe*."

"Dear God," Bret said, her voice a mere wisp of sound. Her body began shaking all over. She wrenched her hand from Daniel's and broke the circle, running from the room as if she had indeed seen a ghost.

Chapter

9

"I'M ALL RIGHT."

It was five minutes later, and Bret stood shivering in the circle of Daniel's arm as he buttoned her into her coat. She had successfully fought back tears, but more than anything else in the world she longed for the privacy of her own home, where she could bury her face in her pillow and try to make sense out of what had just happened.

"Are you sure, babe?" Daniel's hands were firm but gentle on her as he drew her into a warm, comforting embrace. He was shaking more than she was, and she knew that for all his solicitude he was beside himself with fury. So far, thank goodness, he'd left her mother alone, taking out his anger on a subdued-looking Graham. Snarling obscenities, he'd flung the guests' coats all over the bedroom floor until he found Bret's, then ushered her toward the door, telling Graham, "I hope you're happy now, you spiteful little worm. It was me you wanted to get with this masquerade, but it's her you've hurt."

Having followed them to the foyer, Graham now protested, "It never occurred to me that anything like this would happen. How did I know that Iris would—that she *could*—that—" He paused, shaking his head. "I don't believe in spirits," he asserted, although not very confidently.

"Spirits, my foot! Call up the grieving widow's husband? It's the oldest trick in the book, Hamilton. But it works, and you know why? Because the widow wants to believe it." Bret felt Daniel's arm tighten on her shoulders. "She insists on believing it even when her own common sense tells her she's nothing but the victim of a sadistic trick! Get out of my way. And keep Iris Carter away from me. It never crossed my mind that a mother would do something like this to her own daughter."

Bret was barely listening. "Where's my mother now?" she asked, craning her neck to look back into the apartment. "Is she all right?"

"She's resting," said Graham. "She doesn't seem to remember anything that happened."

"I'll bet," Daniel said nastily. "You can damn well keep the witch here, Hamilton. If I get my hands on her, I'll be tempted to send her to join her spirit friends."

"Oh, for godsake, Daniel." If Bret was certain of anything, it was that her mother hadn't been responsible for what had happened during the seance. "I'm not leaving without seeing for myself that she's okay."

Daniel's arm tightened around her. "We're leaving. Right now," he insisted, pushing her toward the elevator.

"It's okay," Graham assured Bret as she sought his eyes in concern for her mother. "Iris is fine; she'll be with me."

Bret had to be satisfied with this, because Daniel was relentless about getting her out of the building without further argument.

In the car she huddled in her seat, unable to get warm despite the blasting heater. "How're you doing?" Daniel asked her, moving his hand from the gearshift to squeeze hers.

She shook her head numbly; then, at his worried glance, she forced herself to speak. "I'm fine. I got a bit of a shock, that's all. I shouldn't have gone to pieces like that. I'm sorry."

"Don't be." His voice was grim. "Be angry, not sorry."

She didn't reply. They were almost at her street. She couldn't get the eerie voice of Iris's spirit control out of her head. "Beware the fire. Believe. *Believe.*" She shivered again and pressed her hands together. Oh, Arthur. Tears began to slide down her cheeks.

Daniel parked the car and was around to open her door before her stiff hands could do more than fumble with the handle. He walked her to the door, took her handbag away from her, and rummaged in it for her key. He dumped Chester outside as he pushed Bret in. Within five minutes there was a fire in the fireplace and a brandy in her hand.

Vaguely she wondered why he was making them comfortable here instead of hustling her off as usual to his house. He had a drink, too, she noticed; he took a large swallow as he gulped down two small capsules she recognized as his allergy pills. He was obviously planning to stay for a while.

They didn't speak. Bret nestled against Daniel, her face against the wool of his sweater, her stockinged feet tucked up under her as she sat on the sofa, staring into the fire. She was grateful for his presence, and for his silence. He seemed to sense that she couldn't talk about it yet. He didn't question her; he was simply there for her, strong, warm, and solid. At some point her eyelids began to feel heavy and her thoughts began to scatter. Daniel stroked her hair. His lips pressed undemandingly against the top of her head. Sleepily she listened to the steady, almost hypnotic rhythm of his heart as she sank more deeply into his arms.

She woke up in her own bed, naked and sweating with fear. Arthur was holding up a heart-shaped frame containing a wedding picture of herself and Daniel, but it was burning in his hands and turning to ashes. He handed her a bundle that looked like a newborn child, but when she looked into its face, she saw not a baby but a cat, with his fur singed and smoking, as if he'd come straight from hell. He clawed her, and she screamed.

"Shh, my love, shh. It's okay, it's okay." Daniel's voice was thick with sleep but firm in its reassurance. He curled around her body, his own naked, hair-dusted limbs surrounding her like a warm, sensual cocoon. She moaned and rolled over onto her back, pulling him down onto her, cradling him between her thighs. Her brain was foggy; she felt scared, and then, in a bewildering flash of emotion, sexually aroused. She searched for his mouth in the darkness.

"I need you," she pleaded. It was true. She'd never needed him so much. "Love me."

She thought she heard a faint sigh just before his lips closed over hers. Pleasure? Relief? She drank in the warmth of his mouth, sucking on his tongue, nipping his lower lip with her teeth. Between her legs she felt him spring to life. His eager response heightened her excitement, and she twisted and arched and tried to draw him inside her.

"You can't be ready so quickly," he protested, resisting. His hands moved gently on her breasts, drawing out the nipples and rolling them between finger and thumb. "Let me hold you for a while, my love."

But she was moving her body in a fever of restless

agony, needing to affirm her existence—and his—in the most elemental way. "Now, please," she insisted. "Just love me!"

He must have heard the desperation in her voice, because he didn't make her wait. He joined their bodies in a long, slow stroke while she writhed beneath him. Her nails raked the hard muscles in his back as they moved.

"Faster," she whispered, beginning to pant. Her skin was slick, burning. "Harder, Daniel, harder."

He groaned and did what she wanted, but before long she knew it wasn't going to work. Instead of concentrating on her own feelings, she seemed to float above the bed, watching the two embracing bodies straining there, snatching at pleasure in a world of loneliness and pain. But pleasure wasn't enough, not for her. She needed love.

She knew now that she loved Daniel. The truth had come home to her sometime in the night with all the driving force of a hammer striking an anvil. Wild and passionate though he was, controlling and primitive and oh-so-different from Arthur, she loved him. For he was also gentle and compassionate; he had proved that tonight. Furious though he had been with her mother and Graham, his first concern had been for her.

He cared for her, of that there could be no doubt. But how long would it last? He'd made her no promises. He was here now, and that was good. But how would she cope when she lost him, when his too-hot fire burned itself out? He didn't love her in the way she had come to love him. He would leave her, just as irrevocably as Arthur did.

"Beware the fire. Do not try to salvage your heart from the ashes." Somewhere on the Other Side, Arthur was watching out for her, warning her against further involvement with Daniel, the man of fire, the man who had once threatened to burn her. The man who *had* burned her already.

"Bret!" Daniel's voice was a hoarse gasp. He thrust one trembling hand into her hair, never ceasing the rhythm she'd demanded, the rhythm he now couldn't control. "Come with me."

It was an order she couldn't obey. Instead, she held him tighter and found his mouth in an attempt to heighten his pleasure as he fell off the world without her. But his body shook afterward, and she knew his pleasure was bitter.

"I'm sorry," she said when his breathing had finally returned to normal. She was trembling slightly with all the emotions of the night. "I lost my concentration."

He rolled over, pulling her to nestle on his shoulder. "Don't worry; my masculine ego can take it. I should have trusted my instincts anyway. All I meant to do tonight was hold you."

She ran her palm over the damp hair on his chest. "Why here?" she asked. "Why didn't you take me to your house?"

"You know the answer to that," he said tightly. "I wanted you here, where *he* had you. King Arthur." He laughed without mirth. "He'd have to be king of something to exert such power from beyond the grave." His hand moved on her, cupping a breast almost fiercely. "Well, I defy him to disturb us in bed." He raised himself up on one elbow, his high-cheekboned face dark with emotion. "You belong to me now. Do you understand?"

Bret nodded, then turned her face away, biting her lip until it hurt. She understood all too well. Daniel was a sensual man. Sex was very important to him. He was a possessive man, but his possessiveness was built not upon love, but upon primal territorial instincts. She was his woman—for now. So he hated Arthur.

"What a damn fool I was," he went on. "Why I didn't

see it coming, I can't imagine. A widow, a seance. I should have known what would happen. My only excuse is that I simply couldn't believe your own mother would do it."

"It wasn't a trick, Daniel."

"Don't say that, Bret." With one finger he turned her face back to his, looking angrily down into her eyes. "It was a shock to you, of course, but you're much too intelligent to let yourself be sucked into that particular never-never land. Of course it was a trick. When you think about it, you'll realize."

She shook her head. "No, Daniel. I know the truth for the first time in my life. Sir Geoffrey Vernon is real. He has to be."

"What the hell do you mean?"

"He told me to believe. That was a code word between Arthur and me, Daniel. We agreed long ago that whichever one of us died first should signal the other, if possible, from the Other Side by using the word *believe*. Harry Houdini and his wife made the same pact. Like you, Houdini declared that all mediums were fakes, but if there were any way to escape from death with a message, he, the great escape artist, would do it."

"I know the story," Daniel interrupted. "He and his wife devised a private code and defied any medium to crack it. After he died lots of them tried, but nobody ever collected the ten-thousand-dollar reward."

"That's right. *Believe* was their encoded word. In honor of Houdini, Arthur and I also used it. My mother never knew. You're the first person I've ever told." Her eyes looked into the distance as she added, "So you see, it must be true: It really was Arthur who spoke to me tonight."

There was a chilling silence; then Daniel sat up in bed and switched on the light. Bret was startled at the fury in his eyes.

"What are you doing?" she asked as he rose from the

bed, stalked over to the chair on the other side of the room, and grabbed his clothes. She ventured a look at the clock. It was three-thirty in the morning.

"Don't go," she whispered as he threw on his clothes. Her heart twisted inside her. Even if he didn't love her, she needed him beside her. Tonight of all nights, she needed him. "Daniel. Please."

Dressed in trousers and an unbuttoned shirt, he turned to her, his body moving in jerks. There was a flush of anger on his cheekbones now, and his fingers clenched and unclenched at his sides.

"I'm sorry, Bret, but everybody has limits, and I've just reached mine. I warned you in the beginning. I told you I refused to compete for your attention with some blasted ghost!"

She wanted to speak. She wanted to tell him that he didn't understand, that it didn't matter whether or not Arthur had spoken to her tonight. If anything, Arthur's presence on the Other Side brought it home to her with utter finality that he was dead. She was alive, and in love with him, Daniel.

"I've tried to be patient," he thundered on. "I've done my damnedest to be understanding. I've even left your hellcat mother alone."

She could hear the rustle of cloth as he finished dressing. "What happened tonight was fraud, pure and simple," he continued, "and you're a naive little fool to think otherwise. Arthur could have told your mother your precious code word before he died, or you could have told her yourself—after the accident, perhaps, when you were in shock. Maybe you raved it to some doctor or nurse, for godsake—yes, that's probably exactly what happened. You told somebody in the hospital, and that somebody informed your mother."

"You're grasping at straws, Daniel! I never told a soul."

"No, Bret, you're wrong. You woke up moaning that

word on the first night we were together. Remember? 'Arthur told me to believe,' you announced. Some secret! Your mother's probably known it for years."

Flustered, she realized he was right. But she still couldn't accept his primary contention. "Even if she knew, my mother would never deliberately hurt me in such a manner. She may not be the most conventional mother in the world, but she loves me, Daniel, and she'd never try to trick me!"

"No? Parents have been known to do worse things to their kids," he snapped. "She's been tricking people all her life. It's certainly clear where your acting talent comes from! 'Sir Geoffrey Vernon' is a masterpiece, I admit. For a few moments there she nearly had *me* convinced."

He paced once across the room, then came back to tower over her. "Use your brain, Bret. Your mother's getting old; she's probably afraid her so-called powers might fail her. Her own daughter has never totally believed in her, and now, to make matters worse, you've got yourself involved with a professional skeptic—me. She's running scared, Bret."

"That's the most absurd thing I've ever heard! She's not afraid of you. She doesn't have the sense to be afraid of you!"

"Absurd, my elbow! Look at the results: You're on the hook, now, aren't you? You believe she produced Arthur, raised him from the dead. A miracle: Hocus-pocus, you have your husband back."

Bret's shoulders shook. His mocking words were hurting her deeply, but he wouldn't stop.

"I've watched this process, Bret," he said roughly, forcing his hand through her hair and lifting her face up to his. "I saw my mother go through it, and I've researched it in countless other cases. It takes no psychic ability to predict what will happen next: You'll want to talk to Arthur again. You'll want to hear all about how it feels to be dead. You'll turn away from living because you'll be obsessed with the blasted world to come!"

"That's not true! You don't understand, Daniel!"

"Don't I? She's got you now. You're her heir, Bret." His fingers twisted into her long dark hair as he added, "She's going to take you and turn you into the witch I thought you were the night we met."

Bret felt sudden rage storm through her, and she fought to free herself. "Let go of my hair! You're hurting me."

He released her immediately and bent to lace his shoes. Then he grabbed his jacket and headed for the door. At the threshold he stopped. "You're a beautiful, alive woman, Bret Kingsley. It's criminal that you should choose to wall yourself up in a tomb."

"You don't know anything about it, dammit! You don't even know how I really feel, what I'm really thinking—"

"No?" His glare was merciless. "I know you're not ready for a real flesh-and-blood relationship with a living man. Maybe you'll never be ready. Maybe you'll hang on to your dear, precious, perfect King Arthur for the rest of your life."

"Maybe I will!" she retorted, goaded into fury.

"Then I'm getting out, now, before I get hurt."

"Before you get hurt?" she echoed, even more furious at the implication that he wasn't hurt already. That proved it, she realized sickly. He wasn't committed to her yet. He desired her, but he didn't love her. He could still turn around and walk out.

"Before I get hurt," he repeated bitterly. "Before you suck my soul out, witch, and bear me down with you to hell."

"That's what you're doing to me, Haggarty!"

But he had already left her, slamming the bedroom door so hard behind him that the house seemed to rock on its foundations. Moments later she heard the roar of his Porsche as he skidded away into the night.

Chapter

10

AT DAWN THE next day Bret was in the gym at the Cambridge Fitness Center, working out with weights. She counted aloud as she felt her sinews stretch and burn, burn and stretch. She worked steadily, almost grimly, using every variation she knew, until the sweat poured off her and her mind was blank.

Afterward she swam, her arms cleanly stroking through the water, her legs kicking hard and rhythmically. Twenty laps, thirty. She pushed herself, not stopping at the turns, not slowing her pace, but her body made no real protest. It was a routine she was used to.

Since her childhood Bret had loved to swim. In the pool she didn't have to think. All there was was the silky sensation of the water gliding over her slim, fit body and the sound of her heartbeat pounding in her chest.

When she heaved herself out of the pool after forty swift laps, her legs vibrated faintly, making it difficult to walk normally. To this, too, she was accustomed. She ducked into a hot shower, letting the needlelike spray ravage her fully exercised body. Gradually she felt her heart slow, her muscles unkink, and her brain begin to work again.

Daniel, she thought, as she soaped her naked body. Her hands moved almost roughly over all the places he loved to touch. Daniel, she thought again as she toweled off and dressed, covered the body he desired but did not love in a pair of old jeans and a faded green sweat shirt. In front of the full-length locker-room mirror she dried her thick black hair, dragging her brush through it, stroking it until it crackled and shone.

When she finished she automatically applied a little lipstick and smoothed her eyebrows into perfect arches, then stood back, almost curiously, to look at herself. Her hair was a midnight-dark curtain framing her oval face, bouncing and curling luxuriously against her shoulders. Her cheeks were flushed with health and exercise, and her green eyes were dark and huge.

Looking farther down, she noted that her body was proud and straight and strong. Despite everything she'd gone through—a dead husband coming back from the grave, a lover abandoning her—she looked as if she were still capable of taking on the world.

Suddenly Bret tossed her head and laughed out loud. The sound rang out, bouncing off the locker-room walls, and she cast a quick look around to see if anyone was there to hear her and wonder if she was nuts. But it was early Sunday morning, and the place was deserted. She giggled again at the thought of whooping it up alone in a locker room. She should be moping around weeping, but instead she was laughing. To hell with D. D. Haggarty anyway!

Then she was angry, and it felt terrific. She planted

her fists on her hips in front of the mirror and stamped her feet. She threw her head back, whipping her hair around her shoulders, then delivered a few short jabbing punches into the air. She moved across the room, kicking out first with one leg, then the other. She took an imaginary rapier in her hand and fenced with an invisible opponent, toying with him for a while, then moving in for the kill with a furious lunge. "Gotcha, you son of a bitch!" she cried. "Take that!"

"Hey, honey, you all right?" a voice inquired.

Bret swung around to see an attractive black woman a few years older than herself, whom she recognized as one of the other regulars at the gym. She was dressed in sweats and carrying a gym bag. Bret grinned at her, unembarrassed. "Just getting my aggressions out."

The woman nodded understandingly. "Some man got you boiling?"

"He's got a nerve. He wants my soul, but all he gives in return is his body."

"Now isn't that just like a man."

"So what do I do?"

The woman tilted her head to one side, considering. "How's this body he's offering? Nice?"

"Mmm. Very."

The woman looked deep into Bret's eyes, then shook her head. "Tell him to get stuffed, honey. There's plenty of nice bodies around. It's the souls that are rare."

Bret pondered the woman's advice all the way home, getting more and more angry with each step she took. It had suddenly occurred to her that she'd been down on herself since the beginning of her relationship with Daniel, believing herself not sophisticated enough, not passionate enough, not *good* enough for him. What a crock of bull, she told herself now.

So what if Daniel was attractive and sexy? So was she. So what if he could have any woman he wanted? How many of them were as smart, as good-natured, and as much fun to be with as she was? And how many of them were as well-adjusted, dammit? How many other women did he know who could come bouncing back after losing a beloved husband at a very young age and be willing to give their heart again? It was difficult for him to make a commitment, was it? Well, to hell with him! If it was so damn difficult for him to love her, *he* was the loser, he the fool.

By the time Bret reached her own street she had talked herself into a militantly good mood. But when she saw a distant figure standing on her front porch, knocking at her door, her heart turned over.

When she got a few steps closer, however, she realized that the person on the porch was not Daniel, but her mother. Oh, heavens, her mother! She'd left her at Graham's last night and forgotten all about her this morning.

As Bret bounded up the porch stairs Iris turned and opened her arms. "My dear," she said, hugging her. "I heard what happened. I'm so sorry. I knew it was an unstable period for you. I should have thought more carefully before going ahead with the sitting."

"I'm okay," Bret assured her. She urged her mother inside and took her coat. "I shouldn't have left you at Graham's. Were you all right there for the night?"

"Of course. Graham and I are old friends. We had a lovely chat this morning. He's worried about you, you know."

"I know. Poor Graham."

"I used to think he was the one you were going to turn to when you finally stopped mourning Arthur. But Daniel is much more suitable. Where is he, anyway?"

"He's gone, Mother. He left me."

"Left you?"

"The end, farewell, good-bye." She drew a deep breath. "He doesn't like competing with a ghost."

"Oh, dear," said Iris.

"To hell with him," Bret added violently. "He wasn't my type anyway. I knew that from the start. He's a bad-tempered, thick-headed, arrogant know-it-all, and I never want to see him again!"

Her mother's pale blue eyes regarded her in silence. Bret sensed immediately that Iris knew every word she'd just uttered was untrue. Oh, Daniel, she thought in misery. Couldn't you have given it just a little more time?

Her mother's fingers gently touched her cheek. "Don't worry. He'll be back."

"Is that a psychic prediction or a fond mother's reassurance?"

Iris smiled faintly. "A little of both, I think. Come into the kitchen, my dear. Let me fix you a nice cup of tea."

"I have only regular tea, you know. No exotic herbs and spices."

"That's quite all right."

A few minutes later, as she poured a cup of strong, scalding tea for Bret, Iris remarked, "We could brew him a love potion, of course, if you could just get him over here . . ."

"Mother!"

"I'm perfectly serious. There are certain herbs, you know, that—"

"I'm not in the mood for any more witchcraft today, please. Last night was bad enough."

There was a short silence. Her mother was absently patting Chester, who had crawled up into her lap and was purring loudly. Chester adored her mother. All cats did. "What exactly did Arthur say?" Iris asked.

Bret put her head in her hands. "Daniel is adamant that Arthur said nothing at all. He insists that it was nothing more than a trick, and he's appalled that a mother could do something like that to her child."

"Do you believe him?"

"I don't know what to believe." Then, to counter the

faintly hurt look that crossed Iris's face, she quickly added, "I know you would never purposely deceive anyone. But I can't help wondering what really happens to you when you go into a trance. Maybe Sir Geoffrey Vernon is simply a creation of your unconscious mind, Mum. And maybe the things you know come to you telepathically rather than from some mysterious spirit who survives beyond the grave."

"There is uncertainty in all things," her mother said quietly. "I myself have often doubted the source of my power."

Bret was astonished. "You have?"

"Of course. Do you think I've never read the various scientific 'explanations' of what it is to be a medium? Do you imagine I've always accepted my lot without a murmur of protest? There was a time when I hated and fought my destiny. When I was about your age I wanted nothing more in life to be normal, ordinary, and as free of psychic power as everybody else." She set Chester down on the floor and took her daughter's hands in hers. "But there are some things you can't change, darling, and it only breaks your heart and health to try. I can't change the fact that I see, hear, and know things that other people cannot see, hear, and know. And you can't change the fact that your husband is dead and that you love another man."

Bret squeezed her mother's hands. "I know," she said softly.

"Nobody can verify what happens after death," her mother added. "Life is the only thing we're sure of. You have to love life, Bret."

Bret smiled, her green eyes sparkling. "I've always believed that, Mum. I'm not mourning Arthur anymore. You're right: I love Daniel, but perhaps it just wasn't meant to be. Arthur—if it was Arthur—was warning me against him last night."

Iris seemed puzzled. "Are you certain of that?"

"Pretty certain. 'Beware the fire.' Daniel's the fire, Mum. You know the spirits always speak metaphorically."

"It's a puzzle sometimes, what the spirits really mean." She frowned at Bret. "Don't presume too much. The 'fire' may refer to something else entirely."

"Well, whatever it means, Daniel's gone, and he's not likely to come back. He doesn't love me, and he no longer wants to have anything to do with a kook who talks to ghosts. He hated that from the start." She dropped her mother's hands to rise and pace about the kitchen. "I wouldn't put it past him to come after you now, Mum," she went on. "I was the only thing preventing him. He's been at me about interviewing you ever since I met him. He wants to put you on *Facts and Fantasy* and make a laughingstock out of you."

"Really?" Iris's eyes were speculative. "I've always thought it would be quite an interesting experience to be on TV."

Oh, dear God, thought Bret. She spent the next fifteen minutes explaining to her mother exactly what sort of program D. D. Haggarty had in mind. And even then she wasn't entirely sure she had sufficiently terrified Iris Carter.

For the next two weeks Bret threw herself into her role at the theater with extraordinary passion. On stage she could forget herself. In the process of becoming somebody else she could blank out her growing feelings of anger and loss. But as each day and each long, lonely night passed by, it became more difficult to maintain her balance in the face of Daniel's desertion.

Secretly she expected him to relent and call her. Surely his hot temper had cooled off by now. Didn't he care enough about her to pick up the phone and ask if she was all right? Wasn't he curious? Wasn't his lust for her, at least, on the rise again? Or had he already replaced her with a new sexual partner?

To keep herself busy when she was home alone, Bret embarked on a project of redecorating Arthur's study. She rented a wallpaper stripper and spent several hours poring over paint charts and drapery patterns, selecting bright and lively colors. It was the first time she had attempted to do any work on the house by herself; she and Arthur had always done everything together. She felt a strong sense of pride and independence as her efforts began to take shape.

When she absolutely couldn't bear her own company any longer, Bret turned to Graham. He was, as always, a comfort. Mercifully he didn't ask a lot of questions, nor did he gloat or say "I told you so." He coaxed her out of her depression, temporarily neglecting his numerous girl friends to take her out. Once he even got up his nerve to accompany her on an afternoon cross-country skiing jaunt. Since Bret had been counting on going cross-country skiing with Daniel, that particular outing was not much of a success.

Gradually Bret began to confide in Graham, telling him everything about her relationship with Daniel. When he had heard the entire story, Graham frankly admitted he was puzzled.

"It sounds as if he was a lot more hung up on you than I'd originally thought. I wonder why he hasn't called."

"It's so ironic. He's convinced I'm still in love with Arthur. I suppose most people who'd been addressed at a seance by their dead spouse *would* be a little obsessed, but I've lived with seances all my life. Even if Arthur's spirit is floating around on the Other Side, it doesn't make him any less dead. I'm still on this side, and I need a man!"

"Why not call him up and tell him that?"

Bret stared at him. "You want me to call the Scorpio brooder? I don't believe what I'm hearing."

"I want you to be happy, luv, that's all."

"I'll be a lot happier if I never speak to him again," she asserted. But they both knew it was a lie.

Each dawn, after crawling alone out of an empty bed and climbing into her swimsuit and jeans in the darkness, Bret stumbled out, half-asleep, to catch the early bus to the fitness club. It was torture getting up, but she always felt better after exercising.

One morning she pushed herself even harder than usual, swimming for an hour rather than her usual forty-five minutes. She lost count of the number of laps. It didn't matter if she ached all over; she wanted to ache today. It was her birthday, and she had no one to share it with and nothing to celebrate.

She hadn't seen Daniel Haggarty for two and a half weeks. She hadn't called, and neither had he.

She'd lost weight. Millicent, the head costumer at New Cambridge Rep, had complained only yesterday that Bret's costumes no longer fit properly and would have to be taken in. Her appetite just wasn't the same now that there was no Daniel to enjoy huge, hearty meals with.

After her swim she dressed quickly, grabbed her gym bag, and walked out into the sun. As always, she cast a quick glance at the spot where Daniel had lounged beside his car on the morning he'd ambushed her. She still half expected to find the witch-hunter stalking her again. She couldn't quite get herself to believe that their affair was really over.

No car, no Daniel. After scowling at the empty parking space, she jogged all the way home.

The phone was ringing when she unlocked her door. Scooping up Chester under one arm, she answered it.

"Bret? Darling, is that you?" Her mother's voice

crackled over the wire. "Happy birthday, dear."

"Thanks, Mum. How are you?"

"As well as can be expected, dear, considering the fact that I have a thirty-year-old daughter."

"I'm twenty-nine today, Mother."

"Are you really? Imagine. Do you have a cold, darling? Your voice sounds huskier than usual. This is still a very unstable period for you, according to all the indications. I certainly hope you're taking good care of yourself."

"I'm fine," Bret assured her. "What are you up to today?"

"Well, darling, I was trying to bake you a cake, but it's difficult with these video people hanging about. One gets a little tired of having to look nice for the camera all the time. I was quite shy the first time they stuck that microphone at me and told me to watch the camera with the little red light on. I could hardly answer the questions at first, but after a while, of course, I relaxed and felt quite my old self again."

"Mother! What video people?" Bret could feel her blood pressure soar. "Is Daniel Haggarty there with you, dammit?"

"Yes, he's right here, darling. Would you like to speak to him?"

"Oh, dear God! I certainly would."

"Hello, darling," said Daniel. "Happy birthday."

She tried to ignore the thrill his voice sent through her. "What the hell are you doing there?" she snapped.

"Interviewing your mother," he answered dryly. "I'm doing a program on spiritualism. Or had you forgotten?"

"Who gave you permission, Haggarty? Certainly not me. I don't believe it! How could you, Daniel?" She sputtered to a halt, adding, "You are really low."

"I've got some really interesting tapes," he went on in a pleasant, conversational tone. "And since your mother gave me her permission, I've broken no promises."

Bret muttered a four-letter word. There was a distinct taunt in Daniel's voice as he added, "Would you believe I'm actually starting to like her? She's a charming woman, and so entertaining on camera. And her history! Imagine how excited our viewers will be when they hear that she's a reincarnation of Merlin the Magician."

"Shut up. She'll hear you."

"She likes me," he said, unconcerned. "Speaking of Merlin, how is dear King Arthur?"

Only the fact that her woolly brained mother was at D. D. Haggarty's mercy prevented Bret from slamming down the phone.

"Damn you! You leave my mother alone. If you insist on sharpening your claws on somebody, let it be me. My mother's almost seventy years old, and she was never all there even when she was my age. Does it make you feel powerful, setting up an old woman for ridicule?"

"The tapes are quite good," he answered in the same maddeningly polite tone. "I'll show them to you soon. Tonight, perhaps. The crew is packing up now, and we should have them ready to roll by this evening. They'll be rough, of course, unedited, but you'll be able to get an idea. Why don't I stop by your place after the play? You have to work tonight, don't you? You might even take pity on me and cook me a midnight supper."

She understood instantly what he was demanding. Her face flushed, and her stomach muscles tightened, sending a warm flood of feeling up into her breasts and out along her limbs. She could hardly believe it. Daniel still wanted her after all. He wanted her enough to blackmail her with her mother's interview.

"Are you by any chance offering to trade those tapes for a date with me?"

She thought she heard him swallow, but his answer was harsh. "What an ego. Do you really think you can bribe me with that sweet body of yours?"

"A date, I said. My body wasn't included in the bribe."

Damn right, she added to herself. He was going to have to feel a lot more than simple lust for her before she handed her body over to him so easily again.

"A date, huh? No, darling, I think the stakes should be a little higher than that. The material I've got on this tape is terrific. I'd want an entire night with you, at the very least."

His sexy tone was making her blood run riot again. She had to draw a deep breath and clear her throat before she could answer. "You left me, Daniel. You're the one who walked out of my bedroom and out of my life. I took a big chance on you, and I lost. There's no way I'm going to give myself into your not-very-reliable *keeping* again."

There followed a silence she couldn't interpret; then he said slowly, "I miss you, Bret. I can't work, I can't sleep. Ghost or no ghost, I want you back."

"Let's leave the ghosts out of it, Haggarty, okay? This is between you and me. I deserve something better than the way you've treated me. If you come tonight, we'll talk about it. But that's all we'll do."

She thought she heard a teasing note in his voice as he retorted, "I don't know why you think you can dictate terms to me, witch. I've got the tapes, remember?" He lowered his voice as he added, "We can talk all you want, but after we finish talking, we go to bed together and make slow, delicious love for the rest of the night."

Bret could hardly breathe, her chest was so tight. His husky voice was sending arrows of sexual arousal through her. How she wanted him! "Is my mother listening to this conversation?" she managed to ask.

"No. She went into the kitchen to make me a cup of herb tea."

"I still can't believe you'd do this to her, Daniel."

"To you, Bret. I'm doing it to you." His voice caressed her roughly in a way that reminded her of the night they had met, she and the witch-hunter. And suddenly, as she had on that memorable night, she laughed at him, gaily, spontaneously.

"I'll see you later," she said. "Give my mother my love."

"I'd rather keep it for myself," he muttered before hanging up.

Pondering his words, Bret wandered around the first floor of her house, absently picking up the latest things knocked over by Chester's ravaging tail. Did he mean that? No, surely not. If he'd wanted her love, he would have been more patient, more understanding. He wouldn't have walked out on her the way he had. And he certainly wouldn't have gone after her mother in this despicable manner.

She hardened her heart and tried to stifle the wild excitement she was feeling. She forced herself to remember him as he had been on the night they had met: dark, brooding, satanic. The Scorpio brooder. What she really ought to do tonight, she told herself, was not come home at all.

Chapter

11

BRET ALMOST DIDN'T go home that night. After the play Graham, who knew the date and time of everybody's birth, surprised her backstage in the greenroom with a party. She had more to drink than she was accustomed to, and before long she was giggling at everything everybody said, funny or not. It got late, and most of the cast members left, but Bret and Graham were still there, toasting each other merrily. Bret went to get herself another cup of punch and stirred the bowl, murmuring an incantation from Act IV: "'And now about the cauldron sing/Like elves and fairies in a ring/Enchanting all that you put in.'"

Graham laughed, saying, "Thank heaven Paul isn't still here to hear you. Still, you'd better do the exorcism before you leave."

"What nonsense. I'm not superstitious."

"Nevertheless, you don't want any disasters to befall you. Your stars are in a somewhat precarious position today anyway."

"Meaning what?"

"Misfortune, followed by great happiness," he intoned.

"You're full of it, Graham, you know that?"

"The stars don't lie."

"Maybe not, but I don't think you're the ultimate authority on the stars."

"Do the exorcism, for heaven's sake. 'There are many things on heaven and earth, Horatio . . .'"

"How come it's okay to quote from *Hamlet* and not from *Macbeth* . . . Whoops!"

"Oh, Lord," Graham moaned. "Naming the play, too. You're calling double doom upon yourself, Bret Kingsley."

Remembering what awaited her at home, Bret decided to do the exorcism after all. The last thing she needed was any more misfortune where Daniel was concerned.

Resolutely, she opened the door to the corridor so she could knock thrice and reenter. Instead, she took one look and slammed it shut again.

"What's the matter?" Graham asked.

Getting a grip on herself, Bret opened the door once again. There on the threshold stood D. D. Haggarty, lounging against the doorjamb in the same insolent manner he'd adopted on the night they'd met. He was dressed all in black, looking like a devil in his leather bomber jacket and a pair of skintight jeans. A very sexy devil.

Bret swallowed and continued her reckless quotations. "'By the pricking of my thumbs/Something wicked this way comes.' Hi, Daniel. You want some cake?"

"You're late," was the lazy reply.

"What are you doing here?" Graham demanded,

charging over to where Bret and Daniel stood, staring each other down, at the door.

Daniel ignored him, looking only at Bret. "I got sick of sitting around on your front porch, witch. What's the matter—afraid to come home?"

Bret looked him straight in the eye. "Terrified," she murmured, raising her eyebrows in mock fear.

Daniel glanced from her eyes to the empty punch cup in her hand. "You're drunk."

"A little. It's my birthday. We've been having a party. I'm sorry I kept you waiting, Haggarty." She bowed deeply, as if to a monarch. "Pray forgive your humble servant for her grievous sin."

Graham turned to Bret. "What do you mean, kept him waiting? Surely you hadn't agreed to see him again?"

Bret stared at her lover a couple of feet away from her and knew that she'd see him again and again, whenever he wanted her. So much for her resolutions. He had only to look at her and she craved his touch.

She drank in the sight of his crisp black hair, slightly ruffled from the wind, his broad shoulders and long, muscular legs. The tight jeans molded to his thighs in a manner that did little to conceal his blatant masculinity. She stared at his hands, long-fingered and sensitive, his fine dark eyes, his aggressive thrust of a nose, his sensually curving mouth. She fixed her gaze on his mouth, remembering. She could hardly breathe with her consciousness of the sheer physical presence of him.

"Yes, actually, I had," she answered Graham, not taking her eyes off Daniel. She could not fail to note the gleam of satisfaction behind his thick lashes. He was smiling confidently, in the manner of a man who knows he's going to get exactly what he wants.

"You're crazy, Bret. I thought you were just starting to get yourself together after the way this devil walked out on you—"

"Hamilton," Daniel interrupted, looking at Graham for the first time. "Do me a favor for once, and don't interfere in what doesn't concern you."

Bret was conscious of Graham bristling beside her, and she automatically put her hand over one of his. Daniel's eyes narrowed to dark slits. "You two alone here?" he demanded.

"Don't start, Daniel," Bret warned. "You've forfeited the right to be possessive. You walked out on me. I could be sleeping with every man in the cast, and it wouldn't be any of your damn business."

A muscle worked in Daniel's jaw, but before he could say anything more on the subject, Bret moved over to the table where the punch bowl was. "Want some cake?" she repeated. "It's delicious." She helped herself to another piece, stuffing it into her mouth and licking chocolate frosting off her fingers with great zest.

Daniel grinned as he watched her eat, looking relaxed for the first time since he'd walked in. "Bring me home a piece. I'll eat it later. I've got other appetites to satisfy first."

Bret laughed nervously while Graham scowled. "You're out of your head, Kingsley. The guy makes you miserable for almost three weeks—you lose weight, you flub your lines—"

"I never flub my lines!"

"You mope around here like a kitten that's lost its mother, all because you're hopelessly in love with a son-of-a-bitch playboy who blows you away in bed but doesn't give two pins for you out of the sack. And then the moment the bastard walks back into your life with an appetite to satisfy, you fall into his arms."

Bret turned on him, furious with him for betraying to Daniel how wretched she'd been feeling. "For pity's sake, Graham! Will you please shut up?"

Daniel had gone curiously still. "Is that true? You're hopelessly in love with me?"

"No! I'd have to be out of my head to be in love with a man like you."

Daniel moved easily across the room toward her, trapping her in front of the table, his gaze drifting over her casual jeans, leg warmers, and jersey top. His attention shifted to her face, dwelling overly long on her eyes, which she knew were underscored by shadows. "You have lost weight. In fact, you look like hell," he added with a Scorpio's blatant honesty.

"Thanks a lot." She felt as if the two men were ganging up on her somehow, particularly when she saw Graham shoot Daniel a careful, reassessing look.

"Aren't you sleeping?" Daniel asked more gently. "You still having nightmares about Arthur?"

"Any nightmares I have are about you."

Daniel raised his eyebrows and smiled. He jerked her coat down from the hanger behind the table and held it out for her. As she thrust her arms into the sleeves, he pulled it closed across her chest, not touching her, but making her burn as if he had. "We'll have to do something about that. Come on. Let's go."

Bret slipped out of the circle of his arms to embrace Graham, who had nothing to say for once. "Thanks for the cake and the party and all. You're a darling."

"Take care of yourself, luv," he murmured, kissing her cheek.

It wasn't until she had settled into the warmth of Daniel's Porsche that Bret recalled she had never gotten around to completing the exorcism.

Daniel stood beside her on the front porch as she manipulated her door key, one of his arms braced against the doorjamb over her head. When the lock gave, Bret turned to him, scrunching back against the door in full retreat. "I trust you remember what I said on the phone. If I invite you in, it's only because we have to talk things over."

"The vampire only needs an invitation the first time. After that he can enter at will."

"Don't be funny."

He pushed the door open with the flat of his hand. "I'm not making any promises. We'll talk and then—"

"You never make any promises, do you? Or if you do, you're careful to tack on an escape clause, as you did with the promise about my mother. Which reminds me, where are the video tapes?"

He pushed her inside and switched on the front hall light. Chester was right there, meowing a welcome to Bret and rubbing his ample body against her legs. He lifted his head and cast a hostile look at Daniel. Daniel stuck out his tongue at him. "In the trunk of my car. I'm holding them hostage until I see whether or not you're going to live up to your end of the bargain."

"We didn't make any blasted bargain!"

"Stop yelling. We're off to a great start, aren't we? Bret and Daniel, loving adversaries."

"Adversaries, yes. Loving, no, " she snapped as she flung off her coat.

"Loving," he repeated. He snagged her wrist and pulled her into his arms. Her breath came out in a tiny "uumph" as she crashed against his chest. Then her breathing all but stopped as he dipped his head and kissed her.

It began all over again—the bursting colors, the melting bones. His lips were firm and warm, his tongue gently arousing as it slipped past her teeth into the soft interior of her mouth. She yielded instantly, obeying the special command of his body to hers; she opened to him, pressing her breasts against his hard chest, arching her head back as his mouth moved passionately along her throat.

I love you, I love you, beat the rhythms of her blood as his hands moved on her, sliding over muscles that shifted and shivered to the pleasure of hardness meeting softness, male meeting female. She sighed with pleasure. It had been so long, and she needed him so much.

When his fingers closed fiercely over her breasts, she moaned, "I love you, Daniel," then froze as she realized she'd said it aloud.

"Mmm, me, too. I love you, Bret," he muttered, his mouth coming back up to take hers again. "I've been in hell, missing you."

"Don't do this to me!" she cried, pushing hard with the palms of her hands against the buttery texture of his leather jacket. "Don't say that when all you want from me is sex. That's all you've ever wanted from me."

"Don't be ridiculous; you know that's not true." His hands imprisoned her wrists, pulling her arms around him. When he let her go, her arms stayed there, clasped behind his neck. He lifted her from the waist, forcing her legs around him, too, then carried her into the living room and set her down on the sofa. Dropping to the floor, he knelt between her thighs, caressing her breasts with tender, beguiling fingers.

She whimpered in an anguish of desire. Her blood was dancing for him, but she had to have it out with him now, before things went any further. "What's the matter—couldn't you get anybody else?" she asked bitterly. "Are you so eager for a woman that you'll venture into a witch's bed?"

His hands moved up to cup her face with a pressure that came close to pain. "I don't want anybody else. Since the moment I first laid eyes on you, Bret Kingsley, all other women have ceased to exist for me. I'll never want anybody but you."

"Don't, Daniel. Don't lie to me! I'm not foolish enough to listen to passionate declarations from a man who hasn't had sex in two and a half weeks. It's like going shopping when you're hungry: Everything in the store looks delicious, but when you get home, you're stuck with a bagful of junk."

Daniel threw back his head and laughed. Glaring at him, Bret tried to untangle herself, but despite his hilarity, he held her fast. "A bagful of junk? Is that what you think you are to me, you idiot? Listen to me, woman. I love you. If you don't believe it from a man who hasn't had sex in two and a half weeks, get your damn clothes off and give me some sex so I can repeat it to you afterward."

Bret stopped squirming to blink her eyes at him. "Don't say that, Daniel," she repeated. "Don't say 'I love you.'"

"Why not? Don't you love me, too?"

She blinked even harder as her eyes misted over. "Yes," she whispered. "But I thought it was unrequited."

He shook his head solemnly, but there was a smile on his lips. "Some mind reader you are. It's requited. Very much so."

"I never claimed to be a mind reader, dammit! Why didn't you tell me? I told *you*."

"Yes, I remember," he said with a chuckle. "Unfortunately, I didn't know whether or not to believe you. You were under a certain amount of pressure when you said it." He moved his hips against her to indicate the sort of pressure he meant.

"Yes, so I was, you ruthless, domineering son of a—"

"Shh. Concentrate on my good points. I'm honest, remember. And constant. When I make a friend, the tie endures for life. You're the friend of my heart, Bret. You're the groove my erratic heartline has finally settled into. I love you. I never want to be with anyone but you."

Bret longed to believe him but couldn't quite. "I don't understand this, Haggarty. The last I heard, you never wanted to see me again. You walked out on me, determined to go 'before you got hurt.'"

"Mere bravado. I was dying inside. I loved you from the beginning, or from damn near the beginning. I felt it the first time we slept together. Didn't you? It was different with you. Something wonderful. Something rare."

"Good grief!" she said, beginning to gauge the depth of their misunderstanding. "If you felt that way, why didn't you tell me?"

"I tried to. I started to say that although it was hard for me to make a commitment to a woman, I felt ready to make one to you. But you stopped me."

"We hardly knew each other then!"

"Yes, and I thought you were still hung up on Arthur. I decided to keep my feelings to myself for a while— masculine pride, I suppose. I was afraid you'd shoot me down."

"Arthur's dead, Daniel. I love *you*. I told you so. How could you be so thick?"

He shook his head slowly, his charcoal eyes pained. "That seance terrified me, Bret. All I could think of was my mother. When she began 'talking to' my dead father, she turned away from the real world. She turned away from me when I needed her most. I was alive, for god-sake, but it was him she wanted, him she went to two years later, leaving me alone in the world at the age of thirteen. That's too young, Bret. I wasn't as tough then as I am now."

She cradled his dark head against her breasts. "Oh, Daniel, I'm not like your mother. I'm young, I'm alive, and I'm not obsessed with the blasted world to come." Her voice was intense as she leaned her face closer to his to repeat, "I love you. I want to live with you and bear your children. That's what it's all about, isn't it? Being alive?"

"Yes, my darling. That's what it's all about. " He lifted his head and kissed her hard. "And it's what first attracted me to you: your liveliness, your laughter. You seemed the last person in the world who'd be mixed up in the dark, depressing world of spiritualism."

"I'm *not* mixed up in it."

"I know. I understand that now, thanks to your mother. She called me up and talked some sense into me."

"She called you up? I thought you went after her."

He just smiled, his dark eyes gleaming with mischief.

"I want to see those tapes, Daniel."

"Later." His hands slipped into her hair and held her head still. "Your mother told me you were in love with me, and damned if Graham didn't confirm it a little while ago at the theater. Then there were your eyes." His hands lightly brushed her cheeks, and her eyes closed while his fingers stroked them. "Your eyes told me the truth. Some actress! A few cups of punch, and you no longer hide your heart."

Bret began to laugh with sheer joy. She pushed him away as he tried to pin her to the sofa. She jumped to her feet and seized his hand. "Look, Haggarty. I have something to show you."

She led him into the room that had been Arthur's study and flicked the switch for the overhead light. There was a flash as the bulb blew. "Dammit," she said. "There's no other light in here."

"Here," he said, going back into the living room to pick up a thick homemade candle from the mantelpiece. He lit it with a fireplace match. "Romantic." He grinned. "Now, what's this you have to show me? I suggest you hurry up about it. I haven't had sex for two and a half weeks, and I might turn into a werewolf if I don't get it soon."

"Vampire," she corrected.

"Whatever."

She took the candle and set it on Arthur's old desk. The light was dim, but it illuminated the study enough for Daniel to see that she was redecorating. The beige wallpaper had been stripped off, and the walls painted a bright shade of yellow. She was painting the woodwork white; that part of the job she hadn't finished yet. There was still a faint odor of paint in the air.

She'd cleared the desk of Arthur's things and gone through the bookcase, giving away any volumes she herself didn't intend to read. Arthur's papers, his degrees, even his photographs had been neatly stashed in cartons in the corner.

"I haven't quite finished," she explained, waving her hand at the cans of paint and turpentine in the corner near the boxes. "But when I do, this study will be mine, not Arthur's. I ought to have done it long ago."

Daniel slid an arm around her waist. From the desk he picked up the one photograph that was left, the wedding picture in the heart-shaped frame.

"I'm keeping that," she said softly. "It will always be important to me."

He stared at the picture without the jealousy that had once burned in his dark eyes. "Of course," he agreed. "You're the woman you are partly because of Arthur. For that I can be grateful to him." He kissed her. "I love you, Bret. I love you."

Their mouths melded sweetly for an instant, then turned abruptly hot. He crushed her against him, groaning. "I can't wait," he muttered, moving his hands up under her jersey to capture her breasts. "I'm going to take you right here."

"Daniel—"

"Don't argue."

"I wasn't arguing," she assured him, forcing the jacket off his shoulders with hands that trembled. He pushed her away to remove her jersey, tossing it on the floor, then pulled her back to kiss her. Their heads rocked from side to side as their tongues danced against each other. She unbuttoned his shirt. He unclasped her bra. The pile of clothing on the carpet grew.

"Dear God, but I've missed this," he said as he gently

weighed her breasts in his palms. His thumbs whispered over the nipples now turgid with desire. Every time he touched her, her stomach muscles tightened, and when his head dipped to take one swollen bud into his warm mouth, she felt urgent contractions deep inside her.

"Daniel," she sighed. Her fingers went clumsily to his belt, and his attacked hers. "This is inefficient." She laughed as their hands were tempted to tease each other through their jeans, their mouths to cling, their chests to rub maddeningly together.

"You're right," he agreed, stepping back. A yard apart, they finished undressing, their eyes intent upon each other. Bret could feel her heart beating in her throat; her skin was warm with the flush of love and desire.

When at last they were naked, Daniel held out his arms, and she ran into them. He stroked her gently from head to thigh, then pushed her down to the floor, spreading her legs apart with his strong thighs. "Now, witch, practice your magic," he whispered. Then his mouth covered hers, and he took her.

Bret wrapped her legs around her lover's driving body and gave herself up to his violent rhythm. As the tension in her lower body grew, the clarity of her mind seemed to increase, and she felt his love, knew it for a true thing. And in her imagination she heard her mother's wise words once again: "Life is the only thing we're sure of. You have to love life."

"You're my life, Daniel," she whispered. She didn't expect an answer; she thought he was beyond words. But she got one.

"You're my soul, Bret," he replied.

A few minutes later, as they lay sprawled and spent on the rug, Bret looked over Daniel's shoulder to see two gleaming eyes staring at her in the dim light. Chester was standing in the doorway, watching them curiously. "Look," she whispered, tugging on a lock of Daniel's

hair until he lifted his heavy head from the hollow between her neck and shoulder. "A voyeur."

Daniel started when he saw the eyes. "Not a ghost, I
hope?"

Bret giggled. "It's Chester."

Daniel scowled at Chester, who was disdainfully regarding the two naked bodies entwined on the floor as
if to say, Good grief, now I've seen everything.

"Get out of here, you wretched beast," said Daniel.
"Go find your own female." He made a playfully threatening gesture toward Chester, who immediately leaped
up on the desk for a better viewing angle. His tail twitched
as he balanced there, knocking over the wedding portrait
in its heavy frame. It fell against the candle, which rolled
backward off the far side of the desk. Moments later
there was a loud hiss and a flash of orange flame.

"Oh, my God!" Daniel was on his feet.

"The paint!" Bret cried at the same moment. And they
both stared in a moment of frozen shock as fire engulfed
the open jar of turpentine and, immediately thereafter,
the cartons containing Arthur's things.

"Do you have a fire extinguisher?" Daniel shouted.

"On the wall in the kitchen."

He ran to get it, ordering her out of the study as he
went. She paid no heed. The draperies were starting to
catch. Coughing from the acrid smoke that was beginning
to fill the room, she struggled to jerk them down to the
floor.

"Stand back," Daniel ordered from behind her. He
had the fire extinguisher in his arms, and as soon as she
moved, he turned it on full blast.

Moments later the fire was out, but they were both
coughing from the smoke. Daniel dropped the extinguisher and threw open a window. "Let's get out of here.
The fumes are probably lethal."

But Bret was gazing down at the blackened, foam-
coated mess that was all that remained of the carton of

Arthur's books and papers. *Misfortune,* she thought vaguely, recalling Graham's words. "Dear God," she said aloud, "I should have done the exorcism."

"What are you talking about?"

She hardly heard him. Sparkling amid the mess was the one thing she had wanted to save: the silver-framed wedding photograph of herself and Arthur. Without thinking, she reached down and grabbed the heart-shaped frame. It was white hot, and she cried out and dropped it, then stood staring numbly at her hand. The photograph had turned black.

Muttering his full repertoire of imprecations, Daniel seized Bret and carried her bodily out of the room, slamming the study door closed after them. He took her into the kitchen and thrust her hand under cold water.

"Idiot! 'Do not try to salvage your heart from the ashes—the heat is too strong—it will burn you,'" he snarled at her.

"Dear God," she whispered, forgetting the pain. "So that's what he meant."

Chapter

12

LATER, WHEN HER hand had been bandaged and the house ventilated to clear it of smoke, Bret and Daniel climbed, exhausted, into bed, took one rueful look at each other, and burst into laughter.

"I don't know what's so damn funny," he protested even as he continued to laugh.

"I don't either." She held up her bandaged hand. "When you threatened to burn me, Haggarty, it never occurred to me that you meant it literally!"

"I didn't mean it literally, dammit. And who would have thought that Sir Geoffrey Vernon did either? 'Beware the fire'—really!"

"I thought *you* were the fire I was supposed to be wary of," she confessed. "I thought 'Don't try to salvage your heart from the ashes' meant there was no hope you'd ever truly love me."

"That's the trouble with prophecy: We unenlightened mortals misinterpret it all the time. Either that or the 'spirits' deliberately mislead us, just to cause mischief."

"Um, speaking of mischief, Chester has really done it this time. I'm probably going to have to repaint the study again."

Daniel promptly sneezed. "I'm *definitely* going to kill that cat. Where is he anyway?"

"The last I saw of him he was skulking under the television, looking guilty as the dickens." She handed him a tissue from the box on the bedside table and added, "I've been thinking . . . much as I hate to do it, I've decided to give Chester to my mother. He's comfortable with her, and she adores him."

"No, sweetheart, don't do that. I know you love the beast. I can tolerate him."

"I love you more. And besides," she added as he sneezed again, "look at the energy you're wasting. I can think of a better use for all that physical power."

He raised his eyebrows and leered at her over the Kleenex. "Hmm, so can I."

"Speaking of my mother—" she began.

The phone rang.

"That's her. You see? Telepathy."

"How do you know?"

"I know." She picked up the phone. "Hello, Mum."

"Bret?" said Iris in an agitated voice. "Are you all right? I had a terrible dream about a fire."

"I'm fine. We put it out before it did any real damage," Bret assured her. She was holding the receiver between her head and Daniel's, so he could hear the conversation, too. When her mother mentioned the fire, he raised his eyebrows in amazement.

"What happened to your hand?"

"It's nothing. I burned it a little, that's all."

"Oh, dear. I have a special homemade cream for burns.

You should come right over and let me tend it, Bret."

"Mother, it's not that bad, and besides, we're in bed."

"Is Daniel there with you?" Iris demanded. "Let me talk to him."

Bret raised her eyebrows at the ceiling. "She wants to talk to you."

"I heard," he said, calmly taking the receiver. "Hi, Iris."

Iris?

"Is my daughter all right?" Iris asked. Bret pressed her head close to Daniel's so she could continue to hear the conversation. "You were supposed to take care of her, Daniel."

"She's okay. She loves me, Iris."

"Well, of course. I told you so, didn't I? Was she very angry when she heard that we'd lied about the TV interview?"

A hot flush spread over Daniel's cheekbones. "Well, uh—"

"What do you mean, you lied?" Bret demanded, snatching the phone away.

"Bret? Didn't he tell you? Daniel didn't interview me after all. He told me his show was too crass for a lovely lady like me. Such a flatterer, Bret. You really mustn't let the sweet things he says go to your head."

"Oh, there's no danger of that," she assured her mother, looking daggers into her lover's eyes. "He didn't interview you, huh? Then what was on those video tapes?"

"What video tapes?" asked her mother.

"What video tapes?" added Daniel innocently, his charcoal eyes twinkling at her. "I haven't seen any video tapes, have you?"

"You rotten, scheming louse! You tricked me!"

Daniel grabbed the phone again. "Don't worry, Iris. That 'rotten, scheming louse' was meant for me, not you. I think I'm about to become the victim of a little domestic violence. Ow! She's clawing me!"

"Be nice to Daniel, Bret," her mother ordered. "He loves you."

"He's a rat!"

"No, darling, it was my idea. I told him you'd do anything to keep me off television. I really don't know why though. I still think it would be fun to be interviewed."

Bret groaned, and Daniel laughed into her eyes. "Hey, Iris, do you want another cat? Bret'll need a new home for Chester when we get married."

"Married!" said Bret. "Do you honestly think I'd marry a ruthless, underhanded...*Scorpio* like you?"

"She'll marry you, Daniel," Iris said happily. "I've known that for some time. And as for Chester, I'd already planned to take him. Bret, are you there? Did I ever tell you that Angelique knew Chester in one of her former lives? His name was Blackie, and it's rumored that it was a careless swat of his tail that started the Great Fire of London."

Bret took the phone back. "And you still want him?"

"Don't worry, darling. He's allowed only one fire per incarnation. He's harmless from now on."

Bret laughed. "Good night, Mum. I'll talk to you soon."

"Good night, dear. I love you both."

"We love you, too," Daniel yelled into the phone as Bret was hanging up.

There was a belligerent silence. "Okay," Bret said finally. "Give."

"There aren't any tapes," he said meekly. "I couldn't do it. I went there the first time with every intention of lambasting the witch, but she started talking about you and how much you loved me and how miserable you were, and well..." He paused, reaching out to skim a finger along her cheek. "I forgot about my program. I just wanted to hear more about her lovely daughter. Your mother told me all about your favorite bicycle and your dolls and the tree you used to climb in the backyard, and the next time I went there, she—"

"The *next* time you went there!"

"I've been to see her three or four times this week. Before I knew what was happening, we'd gotten to be friends. She kept telling me to call you, but I was stubborn. I was so sure I'd been right about your thing for Arthur—"

"Scorpios are stubborn, obnoxious know-it-alls."

"Well, you could have called *me.*"

"I was afraid to. I thought you'd laugh in my face and tell me I'd blown my only chance."

"So we were both miserable, neither trusting the other, neither willing to make the first move. Don't let's ever do that again, Bret. In the future, if we have a misunderstanding, let's sit down together and talk it out."

"If we can stop yelling at each other long enough," she said dryly. "I never fought with Arthur, you know."

"How dull." He reached for her, pulling her snugly against his chest. "I like a good fight now and then." His mouth took hers, moving sensuously, exciting her. "It'll liven up our marriage."

"You really want to get married, Daniel? To a medium's daughter?"

"I hunt witches, remember?" His hands took possession of her breasts. "And when I capture them, I make them marry me."

"But what about your program debunking spiritualists?"

"I thought I might leave the poor suckers alone. One of my associates has just come up with some great material on political corruption that ought to keep us busy for quite a while."

Bret was speechless.

"Anyway, I saw a couple of pretty weird things at your mother's place," he went on. "Once the sugarbowl actually got up and walked across the table to me."

"What?"

"Yeah. Then my teaspoon heaved itself up and dipped into the bowl, putting just the right amount of sugar in my tea."

"You're kidding. Aren't you?"

His eyes were perfectly solemn. "Would I try to fool a medium's daughter?"

Chuckling, she kissed his throat. She could feel his pulse accelerate beneath her exploring lips. "My mother said you were changing," she recalled. "Loosening up and becoming more open-minded."

"Your mother's really something," he admitted, shaking his head in awe. "'Beware the fire.' Maybe there's something to this psychic stuff after all."

Bret tilted her head back to grin at him. "I knew you'd come around eventually. Scorpios are very mystical, you know. They have a deep philosophical curiosity about the mysteries of the universe."

He pushed her back on the pillow and leaned over her, supporting his body on one elbow. He blew a black strand of hair out of her eyes and trailed one finger lightly over her lips. "Yeah? Do they also have a deep philosophical curiosity about the way witches make love?"

"I thought you'd solved that particular mystery long ago."

"Uh-uh. The mystery of you—of your heart, your soul, your magic, your beauty—that's one I don't think I'll ever be able to solve."

"You could interview me."

"Hmm. Like this?" His hands slipped over her soft flesh, molding her curves while she arched under his touch. Her breasts, her belly, her thighs, all warmed for him as he stroked them.

"Ah . . . oooh . . . I don't think the FCC would allow quite so personal an interview."

"Don't worry. I'll keep the tape for my own private collection."

She engaged in a little caressing herself, thrilling to the feel of hard bone and muscle beneath supple, love-dampened skin. "You're a primitive, predatory male, Haggarty."

"And you love it."

"I love it," she admitted. "Interview me some more."

His fingers were very busy. "A little more in-depth, perhaps?"

"Daniel!" She giggled, but the sound quickly changed to soft moans of pleasure as he parted her thighs and slid between to take her down that long, slow road to fulfillment once again.

Bret dreamed of Arthur one more time that night. She thought she saw him standing at the end of the bed, smiling a benediction upon the couple there entwined. In his hand was a silver-framed photograph of Bret in a wedding gown. The bridegroom at her side was Daniel.

Arthur gave her the picture, then turned, waved cheerfully, and disappeared.

Rolling over, Bret cuddled to Daniel, who gathered her close. For the rest of the night they slept dreamlessly, peacefully, safely cradled in each other's arms.

WONDERFUL ROMANCE NEWS!

Do you know about the exciting SECOND CHANCE AT LOVE/TO HAVE AND TO HOLD newsletter? Are you on our *free* mailing list? If reading all about your favorite authors, getting sneak previews of their latest releases, and being filled in on all the latest happenings and events in the romance world sound good to you, then you'll love our SECOND CHANCE AT LOVE and TO HAVE AND TO HOLD Romance News.

If you'd like to be added to our mailing list, just fill out the coupon below and send it in…and we'll send you your *free* newsletter every three months — hot off the press.

☐ *Yes, I would like to receive your free SECOND CHANCE AT LOVE/TO HAVE AND TO HOLD newsletter.*

Name _____

Address _____

City _____ **State/Zip** _____

Please return this coupon to:

Berkley Publishing
200 Madison Avenue, New York, New York 10016
Att: Rebecca Kaufman

HERE'S WHAT READERS ARE SAYING ABOUT

Second Chance at Love®

"I think your books are great. I love to read them, as does my family."
— *P. C., Milford, MA**

"Your books are some of the best romances I've read."
— *M. B., Zeeland, MI**

"SECOND CHANCE AT LOVE is my favorite line of romance novels."
— *L. B., Springfield, VA**

"I think SECOND CHANCE AT LOVE books are terrific. I married my 'Second Chance' over 15 years ago. I truly believe love is lovelier the second time around!"*
— *P. P., Houston, TX**

"I enjoy your books tremendously."
— *I. S., Bayonne, NJ**

"I love your books and read them all the time. Keep them coming—they're just great."
— *G. L., Brookfield, CT**

"SECOND CHANCE AT LOVE books are definitely the best!"
— *D. P., Wabash, IN**

*Name and address available upon request

Second Chance at Love®

All of the above titles are $1.95
Prices may be slightly higher in Canada.

Available at your local bookstore or return this form to:

SECOND CHANCE AT LOVE
Book Mailing Service
P.O. Box 690, Rockville Centre, NY 11571

Please send me the titles checked above. I enclose _____ Include 75¢ for postage and handling if one book is ordered; 25¢ per book for two or more not to exceed $1.75. California, Illinois, New York and Tennessee residents please add sales tax.

NAME_____

ADDRESS_____

CITY_____STATE/ZIP_____

(allow six weeks for delivery)   SK-41b